A RIVERBEND CHRISTMAS

A RIDING HARD HOLIDAY NOVELLA

JENNIFER ASHLEY

JA / AG PUBLISHING

A Riverbend Christmas

A Riding Hard Holiday Novella

Copyright © 2022 by Jennifer Ashley

This book is a work of fiction. The names, characters, places, and incidents are products of the writer's imagination or have been used fictitiously and are not to be construed as real. Any resemblance to persons, living or dead, actual events, locales or organizations is entirely coincidental.

All Rights are Reserved. No part of this book may be used or reproduced in any manner whatsoever without written permission from the author.

Cover design by Kim Killion

CHAPTER ONE

"You *what?*" Sam Farrell glared at his acquaintance Vince Morgan in disbelief. They stood together in Jack Hillman's lumberyard, stacks of boards climbing around them, the scent of sawdust and fresh wood filling the chilly December air.

"It was a long time ago, Sam." Vince spoke as one who didn't think the past important. "I'd almost forgotten about it, until I heard about Olivia's plans."

"And in all these years, you and Carew didn't *tell* her?" Sam started to back Vince into the nearest lumber pile, barely noticing in his agitation that he did it. "Hell, no one told me either."

Vince had just announced that Sam's oldest friend, Olivia Campbell, was about to be screwed out of what she'd worked so hard for—her sons too.

Vince regarded Sam nervously. Sam had always been big—one of the Farrell men—and he still was, with strength that hadn't much diminished with time. Though Sam had left Riverbend three years ago to bask in retirement in San Antonio, he'd kept himself in shape. Vince, by contrast, had let himself go.

"I never did anything with it," Vince protested. "Didn't demand anything from her, and neither did Carew."

"She's been seeing Carew," Sam said. "So my nieces tell me. And he's lied to her this whole time?"

"He didn't *lie*. Exactly."

"He didn't tell her the truth. Neither did you." Sam eased from Vince to Vince's obvious relief. "Same thing."

He imagined Olivia's shock when she found out, her anger. Most of all, she wouldn't be able to go through with her idea Sam's nieces had told him about. It was supposed to be a deep, dark secret, but nothing stayed secret long in Riverbend.

"We did it to help her," Vince bleated. "Dale Campbell was a mess."

Okay, that Sam couldn't argue with. He'd loved Dale like a brother, but it was true he could get himself into some deep shit, including shit like this he hadn't even told Sam about. Dale had been a wild man, and everyone had been stunned when he'd married cool, sweet, beautiful Olivia. Stunned again when Dale had died in a wreck barely into his thirties, leaving Olivia with four sons between ages ten and five.

Everyone had expected Olivia to fall apart or at least sell up and move out of Riverbend, but she'd proved that steel lay beneath her gentle exterior.

Sam advanced on Vince again. "You can dress it up all you want, but what it comes down to is you're about to break a woman's heart. Not to mention piss off her sons, and you do not want them to be mad at you. One is the county sheriff."

Vince lifted his hands. "What's done is done. Carew will fix it."

Nick Carew headed Riverbend's one bank. He'd kept it afloat in bad times and good, and was another man Sam had known all his life. Everyone trusted Carew, he of the impeccable suits and easy words. He'd always been a hard worker, an overachiever, and he'd put Riverbend first—or so he'd claimed.

"The hell he'll fix it." Sam swung from Vince, ready to end this conversation. "I'll tell Olivia myself."

"I saw her go into the diner." Vince's tone indicated he was trying to be helpful.

Without a comment, Sam marched down the aisle, seeking the open double doors and cold sunshine outside.

Jack Hillman, the biker who owned the business, glanced at him from where he stocked wares at the end of the aisle. He'd been close enough to hear the entire conversation, but Sam had learned that Jack, as hard a man as he was, could keep his mouth shut.

Sam clapped on his cowboy hat as he exited into daylight and strode around the town square, ignoring its glittering Christmas decorations and big tree. A giant calendar for the month of December reposed next to the tree, with each day in the month X'd out and December 25th in a big red circle. Only six more days to go.

Sam acknowledged this peripherally as he skirted the square and headed for Riverbend's diner.

"Dale would have loved this."

Olivia Campbell spoke dreamily, her coffee cup dangling between her fingers. She'd drifted into thought, reaching into the past, where she'd been young, excited, and happy. She imagined Dale's handsome face creased in his smile, a light of wickedness in his eyes.

"Is this a private conversation, or can anyone join it?"

This dry comment came from the man across the table, his graying hair making his eyes a deeper blue. Nick Carew had already been an awe-inspiring adult making his way up in the world before Olivia had finished high school.

Olivia quickly set down her cup. Nick had secured them a corner booth at the diner so they could talk quietly. Olivia should be making her announcement and asking for his assistance instead of daydreaming, but she couldn't help herself. Things were going to change in her life and making this decision had drawn up memories of Dale and her past.

"I was just thinking how this Christmas would have made Dale so happy," she answered. "All our sons and their wives and children coming for Christmas dinner. The house will be full and lively. Grace has already started cooking up a storm, and the other girls are going nuts with the decorating."

"How are the boys taking that?" Carew asked, eyes crinkling.

Olivia couldn't stop a smile. "They're as excited as their wives, though they won't admit it. Watching Carter and Faith help little Zach hang decorations is priceless."

Carter, the sullen-eyed youth who'd openly defied Olivia when she'd first brought him to the ranch for an at-risk teen program, had grown into a thoughtful, kind man who loved his wife and children with deep intensity. She was proud of him for coming so far. Not that her other sons hadn't turned out well or worked as hard—they had. She loved them all to distraction.

"And now, as I said, I want to give them all a special Christmas gift," Olivia concluded. "One they can treasure for years to come."

She'd rehearsed the words in her head for weeks once she'd reached her conclusion. It was time, she'd known in her heart.

Olivia had wanted to keep it all secret from her family, however, until she worked out the details with Nick. She'd need Nick's help because if you did anything financial in this town, he was the one who drew up the documents. Hence her call to him, and Nick agreeing to meet her in the diner for lunch today—the diner, not the bank, so no one would suspect this encounter was about business.

She and Nick had dated a few times, so Olivia felt a little awkward sitting here—she'd started wondering if their relationship was going anywhere. Nick's wife had passed on several years ago and he'd been lonely, though not seeking a commitment. He hadn't said any of this specifically, but Olivia knew he and his wife had been in love for many years. Olivia suspected Nick was looking for companionship, not a grand passion.

Olivia didn't mind. Dale had been *her* grand passion, and once he'd been taken from her, she'd believed she'd never feel passion again. Dale had left a gaping hole in her life, but at least Olivia'd had many friends and projects to fill her time, not to mention four boys to raise—five when Carter joined them. She hadn't had time to consider another relationship, not that Riverbend had presented her much choice of single men her age throughout the years.

"Olivia." Nick's eyes held trepidation as he regarded her across the table. "There's something I need to ..."

"What the hell, Carew?" The booming baritone sounded next to the booth and Olivia jumped, cold coffee splashing her wrist.

"Sam," she exclaimed, the rush of sudden pleasure startling her.

Sam Farrell hovered beside the table, his muscular bulk blocking Olivia's view of the festively decorated restaurant. His hard face was flushed in rage, his hair mussed from the hat he'd yanked off and tossed to the nearest seat.

The jolt that went through Olivia was an electric tingle of pleasure, a realization that she was very happy to see Sam, who'd moved from Riverbend three years ago, with only sporadic visits since. Whatever Sam was mad about didn't mar the impact of his presence.

She flashed back to the day she'd come upon him and Dale Campbell lounging insolently on the high school bleachers, both trying to surreptitiously consume their longneck beers. Two wild Texas boys with cowboy hats and big smiles.

Dale had stolen Olivia's heart, but that hadn't blinded her to Sam's appeal. Sam had been madly in love with Caroline, *his* high school sweetheart, until the day she'd died. Sam and Caroline had helped Olivia through her loss, and she'd always counted them her closest friends.

When had her feelings for Sam changed to more than friendship? Olivia wondered now. Or had they? Maybe she was just horny. The theory that sexual need waned with age was laughing at her right now. Sam might have gray in his hair and lines on his face, but neither lessened his strength or attractiveness.

"Have you told her?" Sam was demanding of Carew.

Nick's lips thinned. "Haven't had the chance."

"Haven't had the chance?" Sam's voice rose. "What the hell are you talking about? You've had twenty-seven years.'"

Olivia pulled her wayward thoughts together and paid attention to Sam's outrage. "Twenty-seven years to do what?" she asked.

The men jerked their heads around. They regarded her exactly as Adam and Grant had once done as pre-teens trying to figure out how to explain why they'd been caught arm-deep in the refrigerator well before dinner.

"To do what?" Olivia repeated when neither answered. "Sam? When did you get back to Riverbend? And what hasn't Nick told me?"

Nick sent Sam a hard look as though warning him to keep quiet, but Sam ignored him.

"I heard you were planning to sell Circle C," Sam said to Olivia. "To your kids for a buck, as a Christmas gift." He lifted a hand when Olivia tried to cut in. "What you'll find out as soon as the legal stuff kicks in is that you don't own half of your ranch. Dale sold it off years ago and swore everyone involved to keep it a deep dark secret from you."

CHAPTER TWO

Sam hated how the joy in Olivia Campbell's eyes evaporated as he spoke. She'd jumped when she'd seen him, and a look of happiness had flashed across her face, sending an answering dart straight through Sam's heart.

There was a reason he'd absented himself from Riverbend for the past few years. Everyone thought he'd wanted to live closer to his brother and fish all day, but Sam had decided Olivia didn't need the drama of Sam's growing feelings for her. Now she appeared as though she'd actually missed him.

She had, that is, until he'd dropped his bombshell.

"What?" Olivia's mouth was stiff, the word tight. Though an elegant and poised woman, Olivia could be tougher than any man Sam had ever known, and that toughness now bubbled to the surface. "Sam, sit down and tell me exactly what the hell you mean."

Sam motioned for Carew to move over and then slid

beside him onto the booth's seat. Carew's face pinched—maybe Sam was wrinkling his suit.

"It's not me who should be telling you this." Sam shot a glower at Carew.

"I don't know." Carew shrugged, embracing his reputation as the cool town banker. "You seem to have decided it's your business."

"Don't fuck with her." Sam's heart pounded with the rage searing him. "Any more than you already have."

"Sam." The one word from Olivia had Sam turning to her again. Damn, she was beautiful. Blue eyes, blond hair touched with gray. A white blouse under her knit jacket in Christmas colors hugged a slim body that belied her strength. Ranching all her life had given her a trim resilience. "You tell me."

It was a command. Sam wanted her to know, which was why he'd charged over here like an enraged bull. But facing Olivia now, he sort of understood why neither Carew nor Vince had ever come up with the courage to explain.

Sam drew a breath. "From the story I just heard, before Dale died, he got into debt with some bad people. Trying to raise money to run the ranch and take care of your boys was hard going. Short story is, he couldn't pay, and these guys were going to take the whole ranch. Dale got Carew here to have the bank buy half of Circle C, and Dale used the proceeds to pay off the goons. But the bank didn't want to sit on a piece of property that wasn't earning them anything, so Carew turned around and auctioned it. Vince Morgan won the bid—he paid cash to the bank but said Dale could still work that land like always. If Dale ever was able, he'd buy it back from Vince. But that never happened before Dale died. What you inherited was only half of Circle C. Carew and Vince couldn't be bothered to tell you that. I didn't know any of this before Vince told me today, or I'd certainly have let you know."

Olivia sat very still. Sam couldn't decide what was going on inside her—fury at Vince and Carew? Gratitude that they'd helped Dale without bothering her with the details? Dismay that Dale had done such a thing? Anger at Sam for bolting out with the tale? Whatever Olivia felt, she tucked away from them.

Shit.

"I'm sorry, Olivia." Carew's quiet voice contrasted with Sam's gravelly one. "Dale was desperate, scared he'd lose everything out from under him. He didn't want you to know. Swore me to secrecy."

Olivia regarded him calmly, still keeping her emotions to herself. "How did I not know about it after when Dale died? The property came to me. The fact that it was several hundred acres short would have had to be in the title paperwork, wouldn't it?"

Carew gave her a nod, a bit shamefaced. "Your name wasn't on the original deed. It was part of Dale's inheritance from his parents. But yes, it was in the paperwork. Just nothing you needed to see or sign."

"You processed the will and the estate," Olivia continued in the same measured tone. "So, you could have showed me everything. It was your choice not to."

Again with the nod, Carew too damn calm. "I was honoring Dale's wishes."

"Bullshit." Sam knew he should keep his mouth shut, but the words came out before he could stop them. "You were just too chicken to face her with the truth."

A flush spread across Carew's cheeks, which Sam hoped was a show of remorse. "Maybe that's true." Carew met Olivia's gaze. "You had so much to deal with, taking over the ranch, dealing with four little boys. Adam was only ten."

Olivia's eyes flickered. Carew didn't need to remind her how rough it had been to be a single mom with sons ranging from age five to just beyond ten. She'd shouldered the burden without one complaint, at least not in public. Who knew what she'd done alone in the big bed she'd shared with Dale, his absence a void in her life?

"Adam's in his thirties now," Olivia pointed out with the same deadpan voice. "With a son of his own." Named for Dale, his grandfather. "What happened to all the years in between, Nick? Once I'd gotten back on my feet, once I and my sons had made enough money to buy back the land? Why didn't you tell me then?"

Carew's flush deepened, Sam was pleased to see. He was not happy with the man, though Sam had the feeling he himself had just blown it with Olivia. No one liked the bearer of bad news. Plus, Carew was right about one thing —it was none of Sam's business.

But damn it, this was *Olivia*.

"Dale was clear," Nick said uncomfortably. "You weren't to know."

Olivia's composure was admirable. "Can I purchase it back now? Before I gift it to my family?"

"I don't know," Carew admitted. "Morgan has owned that land for twenty-seven years now, and it's his decision what to do with it."

Olivia lifted her coffee mug in slender hands, silver rings hugging tanned fingers. "I'll have to talk to Vince, then." She remained cool, but Sam saw the cup tremble.

"He's over at Hillman's," Sam said. "Was, anyway."

Olivia sent him a glance then pinned Carew again. "I'm not sure I'm in the frame of mind to talk to him right now. Maybe you can set it up?"

She directed the question at Carew, who nodded. "I'll call you," he promised.

"No." Olivia set down her cup and rose, her poise never deserting her. "I'll call *you*. Nice to see you again, Sam."

Sam got to his feet as Olivia slid from the booth and made her leisurely way down the aisle and out the diner's front door. Mrs. Ward, who owned the place, watched her go then sent a scowl to Sam and Nick. She'd rightly guessed that they'd upset Olivia, even if Olivia hadn't betrayed that.

Sam dragged his gaze from Olivia's elegant form through the diner's glass windows to find Carew glaring at him. Carew hadn't been able to rise like a gentleman when Olivia departed because Sam had been in his way.

"I was keeping my word to an old friend," Carew said before Sam could speak. "Dale asked me to."

"Dale, as you and I both know, sometimes had his head up his ass," Sam growled, then he slumped into the seat Olivia had vacated. "Yeah, I get it. Not only didn't Dale want Olivia upset, I'm guessing he didn't want Olivia ripping him a new one either. Or kicking him out."

"Possibly." Carew's lips tightened. "I didn't ask him why."

Of course not. "You were trying to keep Dale's memory unblemished for her, am I right?"

"Yes." Carew's blue eyes could be colder than cold sometimes, even now when he was embarrassed and unhappy.

"I understand that." Sam laid his hands flat on the table. "She really did have a hard time, and we all wanted to help her. But there comes a point where you need to be straight with someone. Hiding stuff only complicates things in the end."

"I know that." Carew's frown held annoyance. "I'd have told her the truth now. I'd have had to."

Sam pried himself from the booth once more, his anger not assuaged. "Right, when you couldn't hide it anymore. Sorry I messed up your love life, Carew. No, wait, on second thought, I'm not sorry. You have a merry Christmas now."

Sam turned his back and strode away, afraid if he stayed longer, he'd shake Carew until his fancy suit unraveled.

He wouldn't forgive Carew for what he'd taken from Olivia and for all the years he'd kept Dale's secrets from her. Sam wished like hell he'd been able to tell her in a less abrupt way, and that he hadn't caused the deep hurt he'd seen in her eyes when she'd left them without a word.

Olivia sat in the cab of her small pickup in the parking lot, the December sunshine warm through the window.

How she'd stoically walked out of the diner, nodding her farewells to Mrs. Ward and her helpers, and made it across the lot to her truck without faltering, she didn't know. She'd put the key into the ignition but before she could turn it, the revelation Nick and Sam had landed on her finally permeated the fog in her head.

She pounded the steering wheel hard as words of rage poured from her, followed by a trickle of tears.

"Dale, you son of a bitch. How could you do this to me?"

Gorgeous, funny, outgoing, loving Dale Campbell. Grant and Tyler most reminded her of him, the two charming all they met, with a genuine warmth about them.

Olivia also knew that Dale had possessed a desperate side that sometimes came out in ruthlessness—Adam had that streak as well. Olivia saw it in Ross too, her son who'd rid River County of a corrupt sheriff and campaigned his heart out to take the man's place.

Not that it had been difficult to convince the people of Riverbend and White Fork to elect Ross. Everyone liked and trusted the youngest Campbell, another trait he'd inherited from the father Ross had barely known.

Tears stung Olivia's eyes and squeezed in her chest. She'd woken up in the night after Dale had died knowing she couldn't let his loss crush her. She had her sons, who needed her. They were important. Nothing else mattered.

She'd worked her ass off not only to keep her boys safe but also, she understood later, to avoid facing her grief. So many people suggested counseling, but Olivia had ignored them and simply thrown herself into the ranch, her sons, and then her work with kids who'd had even less than her own boys did.

Now all the feelings through the years pounded at her.

"Damn you." Olivia dug the heels of her hands into her eyes. "Why didn't you tell me what you'd done?"

Vince Morgan already owned a ranch with plenty of acreage, though he now leased it to Ross's wife, Callie, who ran a rehab place for horses.

Olivia realized Vince could have taken his part of Circle C's ranchland away from Olivia anytime over the years. She guessed his motive for not doing so wasn't kindness or honoring Dale's wishes, but because he didn't have use for the land. The Morgans didn't have to worry about money much, and in truth were rather careless with it. That fact had always annoyed Olivia, when she'd had to scrimp and save so her sons could wear shoes to school.

Vince could have told her, but knowing Vince, he either had been afraid to admit what they'd done or didn't think it worth bothering about.

And Sam ...

Oh, poor Sam. He'd been trying to do Olivia a good deed, which was just like him. In return, she'd showered him with her rage and then left him with Nick.

"And damn *you*, Nick Carew." Olivia's jaw tightened.

"Taking me out to dinner like I meant something to you, and all the while, you and Dale were keeping things from me."

She ought to have known. That was the trouble.

A soft tap on her window made Olivia quickly swipe her fingers over her eyes. She started the truck so she could glide its window down.

"Sam." Her voice wasn't working right.

"You okay?" Sam's deep tones, never smooth, held his gentleness. "I know I keep sticking myself into your life, but I want to make sure you're all right." His gaze took in her tear-streaked face—her mascara must be black rivulets on her cheeks.

"Not really." Olivia tried to smile, but she was shaking too much. "It shouldn't matter. So long ago. Vince never took advantage, and I can buy the land back …"

"It matters." Sam's statement was matter of fact. "Dale—and Carew and Morgan—shouldn't have treated you like a fragile female who couldn't handle the truth. They took what should have been yours. Go ahead and be mad."

"Oh, I am." Olivia's smile solidified, and it felt feral. "I'm sorry for snapping at you in there. This isn't your fault."

"Well, it was nothing you wanted to hear." Sam made a show of dusting off his hands. "I'll leave you be now, but when Vince told me, I couldn't rest until you knew. You deserved to. But I promise I'll stay out of your business from now on."

"It truly is good to see you." The honesty in Olivia's declaration rang true. "Tell you what," she said on impulse. "Come out to the ranch tomorrow night. Ross is cooking, and with Grace there too, we'll eat better than in any restaurants. They'll all be glad to see you, Bailey and Christina especially." Bailey and Christina had been like daughters to their Uncle Sam and Aunt Caroline, who'd had no children of their own.

From the expression on his face, Sam was going to refuse. Olivia should let him and not beg. Wouldn't be dignified, and Olivia Campbell ever strove for dignity.

Sam cleared his throat. "Sure," he said, surprising her, and her pleasure surged again. "Why not?"

THE NEXT EVENING, CHRISTINA CAMPBELL RACED after her daughter for what felt like the hundredth time. The mite careened around the huge living room, wreaking havoc in her wake. Streamers from the tree, garlands meant for the fireplace, and pinecones Adam and Bailey had brought from a vacation in California littered the floor where Emma had passed.

"Gotcha." Christina swept up the three-year-old girl who pressed a chocolate-smeared kiss to Christina's cheek. Grace was baking cookies in the kitchen, helped by Dominic and Faith, and Emma had already sampled some. "Why are you such a disaster area, little Em?"

"Love you, Mommy." Emma's comeback always worked. She knew it, the stinker.

Christina bounced Emma in her arms as Bailey,

Christina's sister, quickly snatched up everything Emma had scattered.

Bailey's son, Dale, was out on the porch with Adam, the boy helping his dad set up extra chairs for dinner—it was warm enough today to eat outside. Fascinating to watch the bad-ass Adam Campbell, one side of his face outlined by scars, slowing his movements and softening his voice for his son.

"This is great," Christina declared.

"What?" Bailey dumped her armload of decorations onto the table, out of Emma's reach, and grinned. "Having your little sister clean up for you?"

"Well, that," Christina admitted in amusement. "I mean all the kids. Emma and Dale. Zach and Faith. Jess and Tyler's Dominic and little Sarah. Ross and Callie with Caleb. The house will be filled with kids. Christmas is better that way."

"Have to agree." Bailey glanced out the front window to her husband and son, her face glowing with her happiness. "I'm especially glad for you and Grant. You worked hard to get where you are."

Christina didn't argue. She and Grant had been volatile, their relationship like an erupting volcano. That volcano was only simmering now, but the heat was still there. Oh, yeah, it was. Grant Campbell could make love like an inferno.

Adam, from Bailey's expression, wasn't much tamer. Good for Bailey, Christina thought. Bailey had pined after Adam for years, though she wouldn't like Christina using the word *pined*.

"Hey." Bailey looked out the window again, this time at a gleaming black pickup that had just parked, a man with graying hair hopping out with an athleticism that belied his age. "Isn't that ..."

"Yes, it is." Christina raced past her sister excitedly, flung open the door, and dashed down the steps, Emma in her arms shouting her encouragement.

CHAPTER THREE

"Sam!"

Sam glanced up at the cries of delight coming from two young women dashing toward him, one toting a yelling, curly-haired girl. Sam slammed the door of his truck and smothered an *oof* as Bailey threw her arms around him.

"Bailey." Sam embraced his niece hard, filled with joy. He loved his brother's daughters like his own, and had stepped in as a surrogate dad when his brother Charlie and wife had moved to San Antonio. Christina and Bailey had been adults by then, but they'd turned to him without hesitation.

Bailey relinquished her place to her sister, Christina nearly flooring Sam with her enthusiastic hug. The girl in the crook of her arm also joined in the hug, planting a sticky kiss on Sam's cheek.

"That's our Emma," Christina said with a laugh. "She's prone to kiss first, ask questions later."

"Better watch that when she's older," Sam said in mock concern.

"Tell me about it." Christina's exasperation wasn't feigned.

Sam ruffled Emma's hair. "Hey there, cutie. How you doing?"

"Fine," Emma declared. "It's Christmas. Almost."

Bailey bathed Sam in her sweet smile. "What are you doing here? Why didn't you tell us you were coming?"

Interesting that Olivia hadn't shared he was in town or that he'd be joining them today. He hadn't said anything to Bailey or Christina, wanting to surprise them for the holidays, though he'd figured Olivia would have told them yesterday. Worried him a little that she hadn't.

"Decided I wanted to be with family for Christmas." That was partly true—Sam had missed them—but it wasn't the entire reason. "Kind of a last-minute decision. Besides, what's wrong with surprising you?"

"It's the best surprise." Bailey hugged him again and towed him toward the house. "Where are you staying? With one of us, right?"

Sam shook his head. "At that nice B&B Ray Malory's wife opened up here this year. Not about to bother you and your families."

Bailey opened her mouth to argue, but she fell silent, as though saving up arguments once she figured out why he'd really come back. "Well, anyway, Olivia will be so happy to see you."

Sam kept his mouth shut about Olivia and their encounter yesterday—obviously she hadn't mentioned it for a reason. He let Bailey tug him toward the house, she beginning to chatter about the things that had happened in Riverbend since they'd last seen him.

Christina, who'd always been more sensitive to nuance, regarded Sam with a watchful expression. Sam returned an innocent look to her and went on into the house with Bailey.

Sam had no chance to speak to Olivia before supper because he was surrounded by Campbells. Olivia had appeared from her suite beyond the dining room to greet Sam neutrally before she moved into the kitchen, saying she needed to assist Grace. She hadn't emerged since.

Sam wasn't entirely sure what he was doing at this family gathering, in any case. Olivia had invited him, but why? Because she felt bad for being angry at him in the diner? Guilty for taking her frustration out on him after he'd given her bad news?

Or was she just being polite? Olivia would never snub an old friend. She'd been so kind after Caroline had passed, but she'd never indicated she had any interest in Sam beyond the camaraderie the two couples had shared since they'd been teens.

When Ross arrived and started up two large grills in the backyard, Sam decided to take himself outside with the rest of the Campbell boys. Grant and Ross immediately compared steak grilling techniques, while Adam and Tyler drank beer with Sam and watched them in amusement.

Tyler had come a long way from the wicked one-night-stand man he'd been after his tragedy at eighteen, Sam reflected. Now he had a stepson, Dominic—who stood right next to Tyler, trying to be one of the boys with his can of coke—and a baby daughter whom her mother, Jess, had carried in proudly. Jess's gait was uneven—she had MS, Sam was aware—but Jess was steady as she held her daughter.

Carter, Olivia's adopted son, stood a little apart from the others. Sam and Caroline had been skeptical when Olivia had championed Carter—*Is she nuts?* had been their consensus. One thing to help the kid and support him, another to bring him home as a fifth son.

But Olivia had been right, as usual. Carter, the boy from Houston's backstreet gangland, was now a caring father and stepfather, who ran Circle C with competence and loved his wife and kids with a deep joy.

Carter regarded Sam with perception very similar to Christina's. Sam drifted to him as Grant's and Ross's argument heated along with their steaks.

"Sullivan." Sam gave Carter a nod.

"Mr. Farrell." Carter always called him *Mr. Farrell* even if Sam was now part of the family via Bailey and Christina.

"How've you been?" Sam began, then the two exchanged the usual pleasantries.

Oh, you know, not bad.

Good weather we've been having. Kind of hot for December.

Don't worry, that will change.

You bet it will. How's your family?

Once the polite opening was out of the way, Carter pinned Sam with hazel eyes that could make hardened men back away.

"What are you really doing here?" Carter asked.

"Your mom invited me." Sam took a sip of beer, a signal he wasn't going to impart any more information.

"She knew you were in town?"

"Ran into her at the diner, yesterday."

Carter waited, but when Sam was no more forthcoming, he nodded. "I see."

Which meant Carter knew there was more going on, and he'd find out what, but for now, he would let it go.

A shout of triumph went up from the grill, and steaks came off. At the same time, Grace popped out of the kitchen. "Done, finally? Everything else is ready to go."

Grace, Carter's wife and formerly a Malory, was a sweetheart of a woman, but when it came to cooking, she wielded her power without remorse. Grace owned a bakery on the town square that did very well, so much so that Grace was looking to expand.

The males of the family moved *en masse* to the table Adam and little Dale had set up on the front porch. Bailey and the female members of the family streamed from the kitchen with various side dishes—mashed potatoes and salad, green beans, and fresh baked bread that smelled better than everything else. Sam's mouth watered, his stomach telling him it was tired of frozen dinners and takeout.

Sam somehow found himself in a chair on Olivia's left, across from Ross, the sheriff, who eyed him almost as cannily as Carter had. Next to Ross was his wife, Callie, who had the newest Campbell in a baby carrier that took up the chair next to her. Tyler, next one down, beeped the baby's nose and reminded tiny Caleb that he was his Uncle Tyler.

Olivia smiled warmly at Sam but was no more welcoming than she would be with any family friend—or stranger for that matter—who sat down to dinner with her.

"Adam," Olivia said, nodding to her oldest son, seated at the head of the table. Adam had taken over that place the day after Dale had died.

Adam raised his hands to quiet everybody down. When that didn't work, Grant, next to him, yelled, "Hey, shut up, everyone, so we can say grace."

Carter's daughter Faith giggled with Dominic, then the two quieted down with the rest of the family.

Hands joined around the table. Sam's heartbeat sped when Olivia's slim fingers touched his, her grip strong and steady.

Adam kept the prayer short and simple, but Sam couldn't focus on whatever Adam intoned. He only felt Olivia's warmth through her clasp, sensed her agitation beneath her calm.

As soon as grace ended, Olivia's touch vanished, and hands sprang out to grab dishes and start serving. There were two or three platters of each offering, so no one had to wait long to scoop out their helping.

If Sam had anticipated a quiet talk with Olivia tonight, he soon knew he wouldn't find it at this table. Conversations rose, the five men, their wives, and various children chiming in with opinions or observations on anything and everyone.

Sam had been away from the Riverbend gossip train a while, and he realized how much he'd missed it. Bailey had kept him somewhat informed via calls and email, but tonight he learned about Mrs. Ward's falling out with her librarian sister, Dena, and their subsequent reconciliation. He'd known the sisters a long time and was glad they'd made up. Also discussed was the B&B Ray Malory and his wife from Chicago were running now—where Sam had booked a room—the old Paresky place. Drew was actually a Paresky, inheriting the B&B from her grandfather. Amazing times.

"Drew's daughter Erica won a blue ribbon at gymkhana this year," Faith informed Sam. Erica, apparently, was just a little older than Faith. "She'd never been on a horse until she met me," Faith finished with pride.

"Neither had I," Dominic announced. "You're a good teacher."

Dominic, eleven years old, said this without much inflection, as though stating an obvious fact, but Faith flushed with pleasure.

Olivia participated in the conversation only a little. She responded when Ross or Callie asked her a direct question, but mostly she listened, and rarely glanced at Sam.

Sam, on the other hand, was called upon to impart everything he'd been up to in San Antonio since he'd the last time they'd seen him. Also, why had he returned to Riverbend? Was this just a visit, or did he plan to move back for good?

Sam raised his hands. "Don't jump the gun. I thought it would be nice to see y'all for Christmas. I still have my little house in San Antonio. I have friends there, including my own brother."

"Mom and Dad are coming for Christmas," Bailey informed him, as though Sam wouldn't have known. "Why didn't you drive up with them?"

Sam laid his fork and knife across his empty plate. "Honey, I love your dad, but being locked in a car with him for an hour or so is not my idea of a good time. He's the world's best driver, according to him, and he'll tell me about that the whole way. Your mom is smart. She reads and ignores him."

Christina and Bailey laughed hard, familiar with Charlie Farrell and his know-it-all attitude. Sam's brother was mostly a decent guy, but then he'd start in about something or other ...

"Time for dessert," Grace announced as she slid back her chair. "Christina, will you give me a hand?"

Christina was already out of her seat as though she and Grace had planned the move beforehand. "Y'all are going to love this," she promised.

Adam rose, the tall man looking so like his dad that Sam's breath caught. Adam raised his hands for silence, and this time his brothers and the kids actually quieted. "Before we do dessert, I have an announcement to make."

Grace and Christina paused by the door to the house, as though they'd rehearsed that too.

Adam gazed down the table as though addressing a board meeting, which was funny coming from the daredevil stunt rider who'd turned Hollywood stuntman for a while. "As you know, Christmas will be here in a matter of days. And the lead-up to Christmas is always full of secrets."

He hesitated for dramatic effect, and Tyler threw a crust of bread at him. "Get on with it!" Grant clapped encouragement for Tyler.

"All right, all right." Adam lost his pompous manner. "The trouble is, no one in this family can keep a secret. So Mom, we know about your plan to gift us Circle C."

Olivia froze, her hand fixed around the glass of wine she'd poured for herself. Sam flashed her a glance, something in his chest chilling.

"Before you say anything," Adam went on quickly. "I'm sorry we spoiled your surprise. But we have a surprise for *you*. We—the five of us brothers and these beautiful ladies we're married to—have decided you won't be giving us the ranch." He paused again, but this time Tyler and Grant did nothing, waiting for Adam's words. "We're going to buy it from you, Mom. So you can have a nice chunk of change to go anywhere want and do anything you want with. You deserve it after a lifetime of putting up with us and our shit." Adam lifted his bottle of beer. "So, Merry Christmas, a little bit early, Mom. Circle C will finally pay you back."

CHAPTER FOUR

At Adam's announcement, Olivia felt the air leave her body. Her oldest son, who'd done his best to take his father's place all these years, grinned at her, waiting for Olivia to be ecstatic. Adam's scarred face had been softened by the love of the woman beside him and the little boy that bore his grandfather's name.

Olivia's lungs hurt, the moment stretching longer than it should have.

The weight of Sam's stare made breath flood her once more. Olivia was glad he was there, glad he knew what she did. He was a companion in the sudden shock and madness.

Adam would need to understand what had happened. But now was not the time to burst forth with that information, not when the eyes of Olivia's sons, daughters-in-law, and grandchildren regarded her with eager anticipation.

"You all are the sweetest family I could want," Olivia said, forcing her voice to hold its normal tone. "But you know I won't let you do it. And shame on you all for undercutting my surprise to *you*." She smiled, pretending tears didn't lurk behind her eyes.

"Shame on *you* for deciding to just hand us Circle C," Adam said right back. "After all the work you put into it, and you're just *giving* it to us? This way, you get something in return."

Olivia lifted her hand as though pressing the offer away. "I have plenty. I drew a salary from the ranch, as we all do. I put by a nice nest egg. If you take over the ranch, you get to do all the work, and I'll sit on a porch and put my feet up."

Laughter rippled around the table. However, as Olivia suspected, they wouldn't give up that easily.

"But this would be much more than your nest egg," Bailey said, rising to stand by her husband. "You could do whatever you wanted."

"Yeah, Grandma," Faith said. "You could go on a cruise around the world."

"And meet a handsome dude and have a fling," Dominic put in with assuredness.

"He's been watching reruns of *The Love Boat*," Jess said, grinning at her son, who didn't look the least embarrassed.

"Or do whatever." Dominic shrugged. "Run off to ski in the Alps or something. Have your fling there."

"You're really fixed on that theme, Dominic," Christina teased, at the same time Emma demanded of Grant, "Daddy, what's a fling?"

Amusement at how bright red Grant flushed at the question filtered through some of Olivia's dismay.

Dominic, again, saw nothing wrong with what he'd said. "Everyone in this family is married, except Grandma Olivia. And me and Faith, of course, but we're too young. I know she's been going out with Mr. Carew, but he's too *old*." He wrinkled his nose.

More bursts of laughter, plus Dominic's mother trying to tell her son he was being rude.

Sam chuckled. "I have to agree with you there, Dominic."

Olivia resisted kicking Sam under the table. She was grateful to him, though, for obviously understanding that this was not the time or place for truths to come out. She'd have to take her sons aside, explain what had happened, and discuss as a family what they should do. But not right now.

"How about we table this for the time being?" Olivia said, putting her authority as head of the family into the suggestion. "I want my dessert."

Adam conceded. "Okay, but we're going to win this time, Mom."

Olivia sent him a gentle smile. "We'll see."

The group relaxed after that, and Grace and Christina continued into the house to fetch the treats. Adam sat down, and talk turned, interestingly enough, to cruises and where each couple would like to take one—though Carter said he thought a vacation on a boat with a couple thousand people sounded like hell on earth to him.

Sam sent Olivia a glance, and she responded with a faint nod.

It felt good to have Sam here while Olivia's life spun around her, what she thought she'd known—taken for granted—evaporating. Yes, they'd have to come up with a solution to the dilemma, but for now, Olivia pressed it aside and basked in the joy of her family.

Sam sipped his beer, looked wise, and said nothing at all.

"Is it my imagination or did Olivia look less than pleased with our big surprise?" Jess asked Grace the next morning as they opened the bakery on the town square.

With Christmas four days away, they were insanely busy fulfilling orders for holiday cookies, pies, decorated cakes, and pastries of all kinds for Christmas breakfast. On top of that, walk-in business was bigger than ever as everyone in town dashed around the square doing last-minute shopping.

Grace set down the large tray of amazing-smelling cinnamon rolls that she carefully arranged in the glass case next to the chocolate scones she'd already filled in. Jess made herself keep to her place at the computer, where she'd take orders, log in expenses for the day, and track inventory. If she sampled the wares at every chance, as she'd done when she'd first started working with Grace, she'd eventually never be able to get off her stool.

"I noticed that too." Grace set the last roll in place and

straightened, closing the case. "She looked like she was about to cry, and she sure shut Adam down fast. Carter noticed as well."

"So did Tyler." Jess didn't say that she and Tyler hadn't spent a long time speculating as they'd undressed for bed the night before. Tyler had started kissing her, and Jess didn't remember much after that. "Maybe we hurt her pride? She's offended her kids think she can't take care of herself?"

Grace shook her head. "That wouldn't be like Olivia. She's stood on her own two feet, for as long as I can remember, though she's grateful for any support. And our idea to buy the ranch from her seems only fair to me. She put more work into it than anyone, she and her husband. Just handing it over for no compensation wouldn't feel right to me. I know our guys stand to inherit it anyway, but that's different. Dominic is right. She should go on a world cruise or something like that, with a hot cabana boy to massage her feet."

Jess chuckled. "Dominic never used to be this romantic. Riverbend is rubbing off on him."

Dominic had been a tough kid, trying to grow up with a father in prison, and Jess hadn't been certain small-town life would suit him. But Dominic had taken to it right away, making friends in school, learning to ride horses, and fitting in well with the rest of the Campbell clan. Carter, who'd understood what it was like to grow up among dangerous people, had been a terrific uncle to Dominic. Also, Dominic loved Tyler, his stepfather, and Tyler loved him thoroughly in return.

"I hope Dominic never grows out of it," Grace said, her smile soft. Grace loved romance and everything associated with it. Carter seemed to be fine with that.

"Speaking of romance." Jess shifted from her troubling thoughts of Olivia. "How is Lucy? I haven't talked to her in a while. Any romance coming to her, say with Hal Jenkins?"

Lucy, Grace's older sister, had been getting over a bad breakup this past year—she'd been unceremoniously dumped by an asshole who'd used her for fun then married another woman. The dweeb had announced his engagement in front of the whole company he and Lucy worked for, and then he'd fired Lucy to keep from having to see her every day.

Lucy had fled to Riverbend, and to everyone's surprise, she'd stayed put. She'd moved into a small house in the middle of town and started working for the local vet, Dr. Anna, who was now married to Kyle Malory.

Hal Jenkins, a bull rider turned rodeo clown, had showed some interested in Lucy, but Jess hadn't heard of them being out together. This spring, at the opening of Drew Paresky-Malory's B&B, Jess had seen Hal kiss Lucy, but nothing after that.

Grace set aside the empty tray and rested her arms on top of the case. Good smells in the kitchen promised plenty more pastries to come. "I'd love it if she and Hal got together. But Lucy hasn't said much, and Hal looks kind of sad whenever I see him. I don't have the heart to ask."

"Aw." Jess rubbed her weaker leg, which sometimes tingled. "Hal's such a nice guy."

"Nice, but no one messes with him," Grace observed. "Lucy—I don't think she knows what she wants. She likes working with Dr. Anna, and she likes animals, but she's restless. She's happy for me and my brothers, I can see, but she's wistful. I think she feels left out."

"I completely understand." Jess had been a single parent for a long time before she'd met Tyler. She loved Dominic, who was the most important person in the world to her, but when she'd watched couples leaning into each other, holding hands like it was natural, she'd felt a pang of envy. Tyler had changed that.

"She won't talk to me about it," Grace said. "Not about much of anything, actually. She was burned bad by that asshole."

Grace rarely used salty language, and when she did, it meant she was very angry. The asshole in question had better never show his face in Riverbend or Grace might tear it off. Of course, the Malory brothers would then kick his butt, and the Campbell brothers would join in, because they now considered Lucy their sister-in-law via Grace.

"Well, don't tell her I asked," Jess said. "I was hoping, but let's leave her alone."

"It's hard for me to do that." Grace sighed. "I love my sister and I want her to be happy, but I guess you can't live people's lives for them."

"Many people try." Jess had been told constantly what to do by the guy her ex-husband had assigned to watch over her while he'd been in prison. Not so much to protect Jess as to make sure she wasn't doing anything to endanger her ex and his criminal activities. The day Tyler had walked into Jess's life had been a blessed one. "So, we'll let Lucy be, for now. What about Jack and Karen?"

Grace grinned. "Now that's even more interesting. Will they, or won't they? They seem to like each other, and she rides with him now, but they're both keeping their distance from what I can see."

Jack, unlike most men in this cowboy-filled town, was a biker who rode a fine Harley—Jess used to ride herself, and she knew quality when she saw it. Karen had ridden behind him from time to time, and now had her own motorcycle, which Jack had advised her on. Jack not only ran a hardware store and lumberyard, but he serviced the few motorcycles in town and served as a dealer for those who wanted to buy them.

But as with Lucy and Hal, there had been no moving in, no indication they were making things exclusive, no tantalizing goings-on at all.

Jack and Karen were two very private people, and Jess admitted it was hard to tell with them. They *might* be going at it with orgiastic fervor, but you'd never know it from their public faces. Karen never kept her opinions to herself, but details about her personal life rarely crossed her lips. Jess admired her ability to compartmentalize.

"Well, I hope the best for them." Jess curled her fingers in her lap to keep herself from reaching into the case for one of the gorgeous cinnamon rolls. "Damn, I'm getting as romantic as Dominic. Wanting everyone to pair off, have a fling, as my son says, and more than that. More weddings, more kids ..."

"That comes from being with a Campbell." Grace's

eyes softened. "Carter wasn't born a Campbell, but he became one. It's being loved by one of those large-hearted men that makes us all gooey."

Jess laughed. "Gooey. Good word for it."

Jess's rigid shell had sloughed off since she'd accepted Tyler's proposal of marriage. Tyler Campbell, with his dark blue eyes and hot smile, had melted her. Jess had fallen for him the moment he'd showed up at that bar in Dallas, and she hadn't quite righted herself since. This morning, in fact, he'd woken her in the best way possible. A couple years of marriage and a tiny baby hadn't dimmed the passion. Far from it.

Jess caught sight of herself in a mirror across the room, one framed by blinking Christmas lights. She realized her crooked smile betrayed her burning thoughts. Grace's dreamy expression showed that she was thinking much the same things about Carter.

Jess's and Grace's eyes met in the mirror. They let out sighs, and then trailed into knowing giggles.

A timer sounded, its harsh buzz making them both jump. Grace high-fived Jess as she ran past her into the kitchen, her laughter riding back on the waft of the beautiful aroma of Grace's baking.

―――――

S AM ENTERED R IVERBEND'S ONE BAR THE EVENING after his dinner with the Campbell family and inhaled the familiar smells of old wood, draft beer, and people filling space to celebrate or just take a load off. Paper holiday garlands hung around the walls, while lights strung above the bar twinkled red, green, blue, and white.

Sam had owned this bar once upon a time. Then, when things had become hard, like Dale, he'd turned to Nick Carew for assistance. Insurance had assisted with Caroline's final astronomical medical bills, but only so much. Carew had helped Sam mortgage the place, and then later bought him out. That, plus Sam selling his small Riverbend house, had enabled him to clear all his debts and walk away with a little cash.

Sam reflected with guilt that he hadn't immediately broken this news to his nieces, which meant he'd been as bad as Dale. But he'd been waiting for the right time. Had Dale simply been doing the same?

Maybe Sam could forgive Dale. The man had run out of life before he could make things right. Neither Carew nor Vince had that excuse, however.

Karen Marvin, the slick real-estate mogul, had bought Sam's bar from the bank when she'd decided to settle down in River County. There was more to Karen than met the eye, that was for sure. Sam had grown to like her, as had most people in Riverbend. She had a sharp wit and could be an icicle, but beneath her smart business suits, she was as softhearted as they came.

She ran the place well, Sam noted with approval as he took his poured beer from Rosa. He found himself a table in the center of the floor, which sat in a relatively empty space. Most patrons liked to hang around the bar counter or be out on the dance floor.

Karen hadn't changed the bar significantly, or at least

not noticeably. Sam spotted repairs in the roof rafters and ventilation system, with new ceiling fans turning to keep air flowing. Some of the tables and chairs were new but in the same style as the old ones. Riverbenders had been coming here for decades, and they didn't want modernistic furniture groupings, plants, and abstract art.

A man thunked himself into the chair next to Sam's. Vince Morgan. Right on time.

Vince raised his beer bottle. "Thanks."

Sam had told Rosa to put whatever Vince wanted on his tab. While Carew had promised to set up a meeting with Vince, Sam didn't trust Carew not to drag his feet. Hence, Sam's call to Vince, inviting him to join him at the bar tonight.

"You're welcome," Sam said. "Want to talk to you about Circle C."

"I figured." Vince grunted. "Sam Farrell doesn't buy a friend a drink for no reason. I acquired that land all legal and aboveboard. Paid a fair price for it."

"I know. I looked it up. Public record." Karen, whom Sam had visited earlier today, had been helpful with that. Sam leaned both arms on the table, canting himself toward Vince. "I want to buy that parcel from you, for that same fair price you paid."

Vince had poured a stream of beer into his mouth, and now he coughed. He slammed down the bottle, wiped his mouth, and coughed again.

"No way in hell," he stated.

CHAPTER FIVE

Sam hid his anger as he studied Vince, who continued to scrub his mouth on the sleeve of his black denim jacket. Once Vince recovered, he took a reviving sip of beer.

"Why the hell not sell me that land?" Sam demanded. "You're not doing anything with it."

Vince swallowed noisily. "I'm not objecting to selling. I'm objecting to your offered price. That land is worth several million now. You can give me that."

"You got it for thirty grand, which was robbery," Sam said. "That's what I'll pay you and no more."

"Twenty-seven years ago." Vince poked the air with his forefinger. "Land value has increased rapidly my friend, especially around here."

True, developers from nearby Austin salivated over the open lands of River County's ranches. County residents fought every day to keep them out.

"Thirty grand for five hundred acres was a steal even twenty-seven years ago," Sam pointed out. "Carew did you a sweet deal, didn't he?"

Vince shrugged. "Bank didn't want it. I got lucky."

"No, you and Carew ripped off Olivia. Dale too, even though he was in on it."

"Dale got enough cash, don't worry." Vince waved Sam's objections away. "He paid off his loans so Olivia could have what was left debt free."

Almost as though Dale had known that semi was going to total his truck with him in it six months later. Sam had often wondered about the accident—Dale had always behaved as though he were invincible. The semi's driver had been deemed at fault, but Sam speculated Dale's overblown self-confidence might have had something to do with it as well. The driver's insurance had paid out to Olivia, but it hadn't been nearly enough.

"Doesn't mean you didn't take advantage," Sam told Vince.

"Of course, I took advantage." Vince opened his brown eyes wide. "A terrific real estate deal falls into my lap out of the blue? You bet."

Sam's patience ran out. "You don't even like ranching. Your whole family upped stakes and went to the city, and you leased the Morgan property to those shits, the Haynes brothers." Sam's lip curled. No one in the county had mourned when the Hayneses had been arrested and carted away.

"So? That's my business, and they paid their rent. Well,

mostly." Another gulp of beer. "Anyway, I don't much like the Campbells. Never did. Too big for their britches. Dale was a total shit."

Sam turned his beer bottle around on the table, trying to keep a rein on his temper. "You lease that same Morgan property to Ross Campbell's wife, for her horse rehab center," he reminded him.

"I lease it to her because she's a *Jones*." Vince spoke the name with the same awe most people around here did. Callie's family was the wealthiest in River County. "I wasn't going to say no to her. Ross doesn't work with her anyway."

"No, he's too busy being sheriff, a man who could arrest your ass."

"For what?" Vince gave Sam a derogatory look. "Buying cheap land more than a quarter century ago?"

Vince was correct, damn him, that he hadn't actually broken any laws. Sam imagined him smiling broadly at Carew as the two shook hands on the deal. The bank had gotten rid of property it would have to pay taxes on, Vince got land that would appreciate nicely, and Olivia would never have to worry about loan sharks swooping down on her.

"Nice and neat and tied with a bow," Sam finished. His voice turned hard. "Sell me the land, Vince."

Vince opened his mouth to again say no, then he closed it, his eyes glinting in a way Sam didn't like. "Oh, I know why you want it so bad. You want to hand it over to Olivia, don't you? You wanna say, *Here, sweetheart, here's your ranch back. Is that worth a fuck?*"

Sam was out of his seat, grabbing Vince's shirt so fast Vince barely had time to blink. "You talk about Olivia Campbell like that again, I'll rip your head off."

Vince hung in Sam's strong grip, wheezing his unpleasant breath in Sam's face. Not for long. Karen, in a long-sleeved red dress with a Christmas wreath brooch made of precious stones at her collar, was suddenly standing at their table.

"Please release my customer, Sam," she said, her voice even and calm. "Everyone is staring."

The bar had gone relatively quiet, faces turned to them interestedly. Sam made himself loosen his fingers, and Vince sat down hard on his chair.

Karen leaned on her hands on the table, her slim arms hugged by red velvet. "You look like you've about finished that beer, Vince. Why don't you go on home now?"

"Why don't *I* ...?" Vince gaped at Karen and then Sam, drawing a breath to argue.

"You don't live in Riverbend anymore, do you?" Karen asked Vince. "From what I hear, you made a show of wiping its dust from your feet. If I send Sam away and let you stay, the locals will be mad at *me*. They like him better, you see."

"Shit." Vince banged his chair back and rose. "I'm outta here. Don't want to stay in a place run by an icy bitch like you. See you, Sam."

Vince shoved his way through the crowd, people moving to let him pass. Not as though they were afraid of him, but like they didn't want to touch him. A few applauded Sam, then everyone went back to their conversations, their pool games, and their laughter, leaving Sam alone with Karen.

"Want to talk about it?" Karen asked. Karen was only a little older than Christina, but she had the air of a woman of the world, who'd lived through all kinds of strife. She had already been helpful, and Sam suspected she'd make a good ally.

"Not right now," Sam said. He hesitated, and Karen straightened up from the table but made no move to leave. "How about your office at the bank?"

"Of course." Karen beamed a smile at him as though thoroughly approving his decision. "See you tomorrow, ten am. I have a window in my schedule." She drew a rectangle in the air with her fingertips, then turned and sashayed away on heels that had to be too high for comfortable walking.

Sam returned to his beer, giving answering nods to acquaintances who waved at him or raised drinks to him. His heart was thumping with anger still, Vince's words ringing in his ears. But if he could make things right for Olivia, all Vince's nastiness would fade to nothing. Sam would make sure of it.

———

KAREN HUMMED TO HERSELF A FEW MINUTES LATER AS she stepped into the manager's office behind the bar.

While the rest of the tavern held decor left over from the mid-twentieth century, Karen had transformed her tiny space from a drab cubicle with a metal desk and bookcase full of clutter to a plain wooden table with nothing on it but a laptop, and wooden wall shelves with neat bins to organize her paperwork by topic and date. Extra kegs and supplies no longer littered the corners—all those had been tidied into the storage room out back. Tile cooled the floor and tasteful wall art brightened up the place, as did the warm LEDs that had replaced the fluorescent lights.

Tonight, the office also held a large man in a leather jacket who lounged on the room's one chair.

"Hello, Jack," Karen said, trying to hide her delight. She hadn't seen much of Jack Hillman lately, as the weeks from Thanksgiving to Christmas were busy for all retailers, including lumberyards.

Jack unfolded from the seat, his height and bulk taking up most of the space in the small room. Karen closed the door behind her—no need for everyone in Riverbend to watch this encounter, whatever it was.

"Karen." Unlike Karen's young cowboy lovers, Jack never gushed his greetings or even sent her a warm smile of welcome. "I didn't want to grab you for a talk in front of everyone."

"Thanks," Karen said with sincerity. "I appreciate that."

She also appreciated gazing at Jack. He had a trim beard that went with his buzzed short dark hair and brown eyes. Tattoos graced his arms, his ink at present covered by his motorcycle jacket. Jack had tatts on his left shoulder and lower back as well, patterns of stylized and beautiful ink. A few buckle bunnies in town had asked Karen whether it was true he had them on his penis, but she'd only given them a smile. Not because she was hiding the answer, but because she didn't know.

Jack and Karen had gone riding together, or out to eat, and had driven into the cities for motorcycle shows. Once, they'd attended a classical concert Karen had assured Jack he would love—and he had. She'd shared hot kisses with the man. Burning hot ones, and hands had roved.

But that was it. In all these months, things hadn't progressed much.

They were busy, Karen told herself. She worked all the time, and so did Jack. They rarely had time to see each other.

"Wanted to tell you I won't be around for Christmas," Jack stated.

Karen started, then quickly hid her dismay. She hadn't expected the two of them to celebrate a warm, traditional Christmas together with a tree, presents, a turkey, and hot cider, but she thought they'd do *something*. A meal, a sleep-over at her house ...

"No?" she asked, trying to sound indifferent.

Jack's expression didn't change. "Have things I need to take care of. I'll be back in January sometime. Just wanted to let you know."

"Ah." Karen wanted more syllables to come out of her mouth, but they wouldn't. She didn't like how her heart was aching with cold, her disappointment acute. She was finished with men hurting her. Seriously done with it.

She made herself draw a breath. "Well. Hope everything works out."

"Do you?" Jack's gaze was searching, his eyes holding something she couldn't decipher.

"Of course." Karen kept her tone nonchalant. "Why wouldn't I?"

Jack studied her a moment longer, his face giving nothing away. "You keep it close to your chest, don't you, Karen?"

The chest in question was tight, and Karen's face hurt from keeping it still. "I could say the same for you."

That surprised him, Karen saw from the flicker in his eyes. Jack might believe he hung his emotions out for all to see, but no one would agree with him.

Jack abruptly stepped across the few feet separating them, slid his big hand behind Karen's back, and pulled her up for a long kiss.

A searing, hungry kiss, full of longing. Jack's mouth opened hers, his tongue sweeping in like a line of fire. His hand tightened as he held her, his strong, hard body a pillar Karen wanted to melt into.

Noises came dimly to her through the door: the clanking of glasses at the bar, music, laughter, someone shaking jingle bells they'd brought with them. Inside the office, Karen could only hear the roaring in her ears, smell the leather and sweat of Jack, feel his fingers on her neck, his other hand firm on her waist.

She didn't cling to him, not because Karen thought that beneath her, but because her arms were numb. She couldn't lift them. She could only crumble under the assault of his mouth, wanting him and despising herself for that wanting.

Jack broke the kiss, his eyes holding both steel and need. Karen gasped for breath, unable to keep her cool. That kiss had been ... wonderful. Hot, commanding, full of desire.

Jack's grip eased from her as he backed a step. "I'll see you in January."

Karen pressed her hand to the desk to keep herself upright. "I'll be right here."

Jack gave her a curt nod. "Good."

He brushed past her, his body imprinting itself where it touched hers. Without further farewell, he yanked open the door and let himself out, to be swallowed by the noise and festive mood in the bar.

Karen slumped against the desk once he'd gone. She brushed a loose hair from her face and let out a loud breath. In spite of her unhappiness that Jack was disappearing for Christmas, her body felt loose, pliant, and plenty warm.

"Damn," she whispered to the open door. "That man can *kiss*."

―――

FIVE CAMPBELL BROTHERS MET FOR BREAKFAST AT THE diner the next morning, deciding to eat before heading to the ten o'clock meeting Olivia had asked them to attend with Carew at the bank. Grant procured them a table and they all sat, Carter joining them after he'd dropped Faith and Dominic at school.

Adam took in his four brothers around the table, something in him easing. They'd been through a lot, good times and bad, heartbreak, loss, pain ... and lots and lots of Grant's smoking-hot chili.

Grant and Tyler were laughing together about something. Grant was a happy man these days with Christina and Emma in the house they'd built not far from Circle C. Tyler also had relaxed a long way since finding Jess and Dominic, his ready-made family. He'd needed that for so long, and now his daughter, Sarah, had rounded out the happiness.

Then there was Carter and Ross. Those two had a special bond, Carter the messed-up teen and Ross the little kid Carter had taken under his wing.

Carter was now more of a family man than anyone thought he'd be. He lived at Circle C with Grace in their own wing of the house, and he was doing a hell of a job raising Faith and now baby Zach.

Ross, in uniform, was the new sheriff and a new dad, which couldn't let him have much sleep. But the youngest Campbell looked fresh this morning, a glow in his eyes that told Adam his love for his family was keeping him soaring.

Breakfast arrived in the form of eggs and bacon for Carter, French toast for Ross—who would burn off the sugar—breakfast burritos for Adam and Grant, and quiche for Tyler, who dared them to say a word. "Nothing wrong with egg, bacon, and cheese pie," he said. "Suck it, bros."

"Anyone know what this meeting is about?" Grant was the first one who voiced the question as they swiftly made their way through their meals.

"Nope," Adam said. "I imagine about us selling Mom the ranch. She's going to try and stop us."

"She can be damn stubborn," Grant agreed.

Ross laughed. "You say that because she made you wash all the trucks when you snuck out in one and took it off-roading."

"I was fifteen." Grant took a sip of coffee. "She had a point." He chuckled at Adam, Carter, and Ross. "Won't be long before y'all's boys are trying the same thing."

Adam felt a qualm. Three-year-old Dale was a sweet kid, but he was a Campbell. "Your Emma has a lot of spirit," he countered. "I have the feeling she'll be the one teaching the boys how to hotwire a pickup."

Grant winced, and Adam laughed.

Carter checked his watch. "We should be heading over."

"Yep." Adam signaled Mrs. Ward, who marched to them, order pad in hand.

"I'm not writing out five tickets," she declared. "You boys decide amongst yourselves who's paying. I'll see you at the register."

She slapped a bill face down on the table and stomped away. No one reached for the paper.

"Split it five ways?" Ross suggested.

"You say that because French toast is the most expensive plate here," Grant said.

"Sure is," Tyler agreed. "You should have ordered the quiche. Compact, cheap, and tasty. Protein in a pie."

"We run a business," Carter said with a frown. "We can figure out who owes what."

Before he could turn over the check, a slim hand stretched to it. "Why don't you let me get that today?"

Karen Marvin slid the ticket off the table and continued walking to the front before Adam and his brothers could react.

CHAPTER SIX

Adam sprang to his feet, and the other four did as well. By the time they reached the front counter, Karen had already gone, and Mrs. Ward was sliding the signed credit card slip through a slot in a drawer.

"How nice of her," Mrs. Ward said. "Say thank you politely to her, boys." She turned her back and headed for the kitchen, not interested in their protests.

Karen had halted on the sidewalk outside, not far from the diner. The weather had grown cold overnight, which was normal for December, and she was busily sliding thin leather gloves onto her hands.

"You're heading to the bank, right?" Karen asked the Campbells, her voice light, as they barreled out of the diner. "Why don't you walk with me?"

Adam knew she wasn't worried about walking alone in Riverbend. Tyler had once said that if anyone ever tried to assail Karen, they'd melt into a puddle of acid from her basilisk stare. The brothers hadn't argued with him.

Karen started off for the town square at a brisk pace. Adam made sure he strode next to her, and Grant took her far side. Adam did not want the rest of Riverbend watching Karen lead them across the street like a mama duck and her hulking cowboy ducklings.

The bank was quiet this morning, though the rest of the square was thronged with people from Riverbend and White Fork doing last-minute Christmas shopping. Many locals drove to Austin to the big stores there, but Riverbend boutiques always had special things like hand-knits and glass art that couldn't be found in chain stores in the city, not to mention the kick-ass pastries and pies in Grace's shop.

Adam spied Grace speeding out of the shop's door along the square, handing bags to customers waiting outside. More thronged the shop's interior, Jess taking orders, her fingers flying on the keyboard.

Grace paused to peer at the five brothers and Karen, her warm smile flashing when Carter raised his hand to wave to her. Grace blew him a kiss, and Carter flushed but looked pleased.

They reached the bank building, and Adam darted forward to hold the door open for Karen. He followed her immediately, not volunteering to be the doorman for the rest of his brothers. The other four got themselves inside with only minimal discord.

The bank's vaulted marble interior discouraged conversation. *This is an important edifice,* the lobby whispered. *Show some respect.* Whoever had designed this building back in eighteen something or other—Bailey would know the exact date—had decided it needed to be weighty and lofty at the same time.

Adam had never entered the bank without feeling like an insignificant bug. After all, *it* had stood here for a hundred and fifty years or so, watching generations of Riverbenders come and go, while Adam had been born here only a few decades ago. The ceiling far above, held up by stone pillars, always made him squirrelly.

Karen led them up a flight of polished stone stairs with carved wooden banisters to the second floor, where the paneled halls were more normal in size. She smiled at them as she stopped in front of the office from which she managed AGCT Enterprises, the Campbells' nonprofit. Their mission: to make sure local businesses received loans and grants to keep them going. They'd helped Ray's wife fix up her derelict B&B and Grace get up and running with her bakery.

"Good day, gentlemen." Karen nodded at them as she opened the door, slipped inside, and shut it in Adam's face. The AGCT logo sat steadily before his eyes.

Sam Farrell had been waiting inside for her, rising as Karen entered, scowling as he caught Adam's eye. Adam frowned at the closed door. What the hell was Sam doing there? Adam hadn't heard anything about Sam seeking a grant or loan. He and Carter usually fielded all requests.

The rest of the brothers had already moved down the corridor to Mr. Carew's office, apparently without having noticed Sam. Adam abandoned his speculation and strode after them.

The meeting wouldn't be held in Carew's actual office,

because all five Campbells wouldn't fit in the small space. Grant opened the door of the conference room next to it where Olivia had indicated they'd gather.

Carew rose from the head of the conference table as Grant led the way inside. This room had no windows—it was enclosed, walnut-paneled, and graced with paintings, mostly of Hill Country scenes.

Olivia, sitting on Carew's right, remained in her chair. She looked mad as hell, which meant calm, cool, and collected but with a glint of steel in her eyes.

Mr. Carew waited until the brothers had filed in, given their polite greetings to him and their mother, and seated themselves. None of Adam's brothers argued about who sat where today, all of them sensing trouble.

Carter shut the door before he took the chair next to Olivia and sent Mr. Carew, who remained standing, a sharp stare.

"Is this about gifting us the ranch?" Adam rumbled before either Carew or Olivia could begin. "We've already decided what we want to do. Not gonna take no for an answer, Mom."

Olivia held up her hand. She wore silver and turquoise rings that matched her soft silk turquoise top and gray silk scarf. She'd dressed in her favorite colors for this meeting, which told Adam she truly was angry.

"Let Mr. Carew speak," she said.

Mr. Carew, Adam noted. Not Nick. As though she hadn't gone out with him from time to time in the past year.

Carew cleared his throat. "I will come right out and say

it. About six months before your father died, he sold off five hundred acres of Circle C Ranch."

Silence blanketed the room. Adam went very still, a coldness clenching inside him. At the same time, he wanted to leap up and demand to know what the hell Carew was talking about. His dad never would have sold anything out from under the family. Would he? Had Mom known? From Olivia's barely contained fury, Adam guessed probably not.

His brothers sat in similar paralysis, until finally Carter broke the tension.

"What?" Carter's single word held a multitude of questions.

"Dale had run into a lot of debt," Carew said. His voice was quiet, but Adam sensed his nervousness. "He came to me. He had no choice."

"What kind of debt?" Carter asked. "Be straight with us."

Carew again cleared his throat, a dry sound he'd perfected over the years. "Your father owed taxes on the ranch, plus he'd mortgaged the house. He'd also bought a hundred head of cattle to try to make a profit on. Basically, he was scrambling to take care of his family—if he didn't pay the taxes, the entire ranch would be taken away. He couldn't find buyers quickly enough for the steers, and he'd do anything not to sell his family's home. So he went to San Antonio, where he'd heard of people he could get cash from quickly."

"You mean loan sharks." Carter's eyes narrowed. "Who I bet wanted the money back immediately with a huge vig."

"More or less," Carew said. "Dale knew he stood to lose

everything, so I stepped in and offered to buy some acreage. The land was worth more than the amount he'd borrowed, so he was able to pay off the men in San Antonio, write a check for his property taxes, and start fresh."

Carter didn't answer. Grant, Tyler, and Ross continued their silence—disbelief, anger, and sadness flitting over the faces of each brother. Olivia continued to sit stoically, and Adam suddenly wanted to hug her.

"Did you know about all this, Mom?" he asked in a low voice.

"No." Her response was soft. "I found out a few days ago."

"Dad never told you?" Tyler burst in, incredulous. "Why the hell not?"

Olivia laced her fingers together and then unlaced them. "Shame, I imagine. Dale always wanted to be seen as the provider, wanted to be the best husband and father who ever lived. He didn't want me to worry, and he didn't want me to lose my belief in him."

More fury at his father flashed through Adam, but behind it came a wave of understanding. He pictured Dale, the tall, strong man Adam remembered, sitting in Carew's office, having to make this terrible decision. If Adam had been in the same position, he knew he'd have done whatever it took to take care of Bailey and his son, and any other kids who might come their way.

Except that Adam would tell Bailey. He'd be tempted not to—like his father, he'd want to simply take care of everything and keep it quiet, but he'd make himself tell her.

He'd swallow his pride in case his actions came back to bite her later, just as this one was biting Olivia.

Adam flicked his gaze to Carew, whose only betrayal of nervousness was a tap of his fingers on the chair he stood before.

"What was your excuse, Carew?" Adam demanded. "I sort of understand why my dad kept all this a big secret. That was just who he was—right or wrong. But *you* could have told Mom years ago."

Olivia broke in before Carew could answer. "Don't worry, I've berated him plenty. Sam has too. Now, we can sit here and blame and grouse for hours, but it won't change anything. The reality is, Vince Morgan now owns that land. To his credit, he's never stopped us from using it and never asked for rent for it, which is another reason I didn't realize the truth. But that's where things stand."

Adam listened, dumbfounded, and he sensed similar shock skimming around the table.

First, he didn't miss the mention of Sam Farrell that his mom blew right past. Second, Vince Morgan? Seriously? Where did he come into it? Third, why hadn't Vince ever come knocking, demanding Olivia lease that acreage from him if the Campbells kept on working it? What did he stand to gain?

"Shit," Carter said.

"So, the truth is," Ross said, speaking for the first time, "we own half of Circle C, and Morgan owns the rest? What part, specifically, does he have?"

Carew opened a folder and began to pass out papers. The man had prepared.

A printout of a plat map landed in front of Adam, which showed that the Campbells possessed the land that held the house, barn, riding arenas, and a swath that ran west and north toward the river. The eastern acres, including a chunk running along the road, was in the possession of Vince Morgan.

Adam swallowed bile. At least Carew and Morgan hadn't sold the house out from under them. If anyone in this transaction had been a little more callous, the Campbells might have lost the house too.

Grant dropped the papers he'd studied back to the table. "Solution is simple," he rumbled. "We buy it back from Vince."

Both Carew and Olivia looked unhappy. "He won't sell," Carew announced. "Not for less than a few million, anyway."

Olivia nodded. "Sam is down the hall with Karen right now trying to figure out how to encourage him to let us buy it for a better price."

"Huh," Adam said. That explained Sam's presence, but not entirely.

"What has Sam got to do with it?" Tyler asked the question Adam had in mind. "We like him—hell, we've drunk at his bar for years, and Bailey and Christina are two of our favorite people, but—"

"He's been my friend for a long time," Olivia interrupted, her voice strangely hard. "He's concerned. I think it's nice."

Nice? Adam's brows went up. Olivia studied the map

Carew had handed her, gaze fixed on it as pink brushed her cheeks.

Well, damn.

Adam exchanged a glance with Grant, who also looked amazed. Ross started to grin, as did Tyler, but Carter appeared grim. He'd always been very protective of Olivia.

It all might be nothing. Sam and his wife had been best friends with Mom and Dad all their lives—Adam remembered the four hanging out together, either at Circle C for cookouts and beer or meeting up at the diner or bar. Olivia and Caroline had gone for many trips to Austin or San Antonio for some girl time, like the Campbell wives did now.

After Dad had passed away, Caroline had resolutely taken Olivia under her wing, continuing the lady's day out trips or babysitting the Campbell brothers so Olivia could relax once in a while. Sam had helped on the ranch as well, never mind how busy he was running his own business.

They'd all been fast friends, and Adam had never noticed anything untoward between Olivia and Sam. Even Adam as an oblivious teen would have seen something, especially after he'd started having the hots for Bailey—anything Farrell had been on his radar. He knew Olivia would never have betrayed her best friend, Caroline, no matter what.

But now Dad and Caroline were gone, Mom and Sam were alone, and they had all those good times in common. Sam had returned to Riverbend ...

Adam shut down the speculation to deal with the problem before them. "We might need to have a little talk with Vince." He interlocked his hands behind his head, and his brothers either grinned in agreement or nodded.

"No," Olivia said firmly. "No threats. Vince has the upper hand here. The land is legally his, whether we like it or not."

"Just a brief word," Carter said, scowling. "Just me."

"Carter." Olivia took the tone she had back when Carter had been fourteen and defiant. "We need to tread the high road. What's done is done. I'm not happy that half your inheritance vanished out from under us, but if we can't get the land back from Vince, we'll have to live with this. At least Dale didn't leave us in debt to loan sharks or to the bank. The rest of the property is free and clear. Let's be thankful that Vince never marched to our door pressuring me for years of back rent to him."

Adam frowned to himself as his mother finished. Why *hadn't* Vince ever come to collect? he wondered again. Vince would have been perfectly justified to either offer Olivia terms for leasing the land or to kick them off completely. Adam would suspect kindness in another person, but Vince had the reputation for liking money. That's why he'd rented out his own property instead of doing the backbreaking work of farming or ranching.

Something to figure out later, Adam told himself. For now, Mom was right. Pushing Vince around, while it might be satisfying, wouldn't solve anything. They needed to figure out how to go forward from here. If Bailey had taught Adam anything, it was that sitting back and thinking about a problem, instead of bullying it, led to solutions.

Well, Bailey had taught him a hell of a lot more than

that. Adam faded as his brothers and Mr. Carew continued the discussion, some impatient, some, like Ross, trying to remain reasonable.

Adam's thoughts turned to Bailey, her brown eyes that welcomed him at the end of a day—or in the middle of the day, for that matter. Her smile had made everything that had been hurt inside Adam heal to peaceful joy.

———

"You're a genius, Sam Farrell." Karen pressed her well-groomed hands together in what passed in her for excitement. "Do we race down the hall and tell them?"

CHAPTER SEVEN

Sam shook his head at Karen's question. "No. Not yet."

The plan he'd formulated as he'd lain awake last night in his room at the B&B could work, or it could flop like a dead fish.

"Too many contingencies," he said. "I don't want Olivia to get her hopes up."

"I see." Karen sounded disappointed. "Sorry, but canny business deals exhilarate me. In your scenario, everyone wins. More or less."

"More or less." The inkling of what to do had come to Sam after Vince had been such a dickhead about selling the land. Sam's plan would appeal to Vince's greed as well as his distaste for Campbells.

Karen straightened the holly leaf pin that adorned the collar of her red plaid dress. "I'm thinking you want to seal the deal and then present it to Olivia on a platter," she said with her usual shrewdness.

Sam felt his face heat. "Something like that."

"I see."

"Do you?" Sam grew irritated at Karen's knowing tone. "Olivia and I have been friends for decades. I want her to hear all this from me."

"Oh, I understand." Karen's teeth flashed in another smile. "I think it's wonderful that you and Olivia have found each other."

Sam barely stopped himself from rolling his eyes. "We haven't *found* each other. She's a sweet woman, and she's been through a lot. She deserves some happiness of her own."

"I totally agree," Karen said briskly. "Olivia is one of the hardest working women I've ever met. She built up the ranch's business stone by stone and raised five sons who turned out to be fine human beings. I've had such fun watching them be married off one by one."

Sam softened a bit, and he had to chuckle. "I've watched *you* try to round them up for yourself—but you didn't have a chance with Grant against my niece."

"Christina?" Karen appeared surprised Sam thought she'd tried to compete. "Heavens no. Once I saw the way Grant looked at her, I knew there was only one woman for him. Besides, I was only after a little fun. I am *not* the settling down type. Tried it with three husbands. I'm done with that."

"Are you?" Sam asked her.

He had the pleasure of watching Karen blush. The flush started at her neck where the pin was and worked its way to her forehead.

"I most certainly am." Karen came out of her relaxed

pose and grabbed a stack of folders that lay on her desk. "Now, my window is closing. I have things to do. Let me know how you want to proceed."

"Gotcha." Sam heaved himself out of the chair. "Good day to you, Ms. Marvin. And thank you."

"You're welcome, Mr. Farrell," Karen unbent enough to say. "Merry Christmas."

"To you as well." Sam raised a hand goodbye as he left her office.

Struck a nerve, Sam thought as he strode down the hall. *She has it bad for Jack Hillman.*

Jack had been a troublemaker in his younger days, but he seemed to have turned out all right. Karen could do a lot worse.

Sam paused as he passed the conference room door, the thick oak paneling hiding Olivia and her family from him. He was tempted to pop inside and join the discussion, but no. He might blurt out his idea, and he truly wanted to make sure it would work before he promised anything to Olivia.

While he'd love a moment to fill his gaze with Olivia's eyes, her beautiful face, and her warm smile, Sam made his feet move past the closed door and took himself resolutely out of the building.

Lucy Malory continued sanitizing the small surgery room while Anna carried the cat, whose wounds she'd finished sewing, to rest in a soft crate. The poor thing had had a run-in with a rival cat, but fortunately had gotten away without too much damage. Enough, though. Anna had cleaned, stitched, and medicated while Lucy held instruments and clipped sutures.

They finished and took the cat to Anna's office, where she could keep an eye on it until its owner arrived. Lucy scrubbed her hands and moved to her own desk.

She'd taken over the accounting chores for Anna's business, Anna saying Lucy's great financial skills would be wasted on her simply answering the phone and making appointments. Even keeping Anna's books had to be a comedown for someone who'd worked for a billion-dollar business.

Lucy had tried to explain, then given up, that the relatively simple task of making sure Anna was in the black every month was a welcome relaxation. The high pressure to sell, make deals, and negotiate the highest fees possible for the company, as well as keeping Clyde, her boyfriend and boss, happy, had taken its toll on her.

She hadn't even noticed how strained she'd been. Lucy had thought the constant stress and the drama-filled relationship with Clyde meant she'd succeeded. She'd believed she'd freed herself from small-town constraints and entered the exciting world of big business in the city.

A large company was kind of like high school, though, she'd discovered. There were the shining stars—people everyone wanted to be around—as well as those who were collectively ignored. Lucy had thought herself a shining star, popular with others in the business, the small-town girl made good.

Turns out, most of her so-called friends had only wanted to ingratiate themselves with her because of Clyde, whose father owned the company. They hoped Lucy would put in a kind word for them as they swarmed up the ranks. Once Clyde turned his back on Lucy, all those people vanished like smoke in the wind.

Creating spreadsheets for Anna's vet's office and keeping a rancher calm as he described his horse's medical issue was a piece of cake compared to negotiating the treacherous waters of Clyde Gordon's family company.

"That was the last surgery for the day," Anna reminded Lucy once the grateful owner had come for the cat and departed with medication and Anna's instructions for its care. "How about we close up and finish Christmas shopping? I don't want to find empty shelves at the last minute."

Ray and Drew were hosting a big Malory dinner at the B&B on Christmas Day, with the Malorys' mom and her boyfriend coming in from Austin. Kyle was contributing his chili, and Anna had offered to bring pies from Grace's bakery. Grace and Carter would have dinner with the Campbells, and then come over to the B&B for dessert.

"Sure, *you* should." Lucy made no move to shut down. "I'll just finish up here."

She felt warmth and looked up to find Anna right next to her, her abdomen round with Kyle's first kid. Anna was so petite that until lately it had been hard to tell she was pregnant at all. Lucy was certain that if she ever got pregnant, she'd puff up like a balloon.

That thought made her realize her chances of being a mom were fading, which didn't help her already low spirits.

"I need you to help me pick out things for Kyle and Ray," Anna said. She might be a small young woman, but she contained a lot of mettle. "You know them better than I do."

"For Kyle, another shelf for all his trophies," Lucy joked. "For Ray, a toolbox. He's become Mr. Fix-It at the B&B."

Anna didn't laugh. "Not helping. Come on, Lucy. We'll stuff ourselves with vegan Christmas cookies at Grace's bakery, and then buy some of her goodies for Christmas morning. You're still staying over, right?"

Anna asked this last with a severe light in her blue eyes. She and Kyle had invited Lucy, who was renting the shotgun house Anna used to live in, to spend Christmas Eve at the Malory ranch, sleeping in her old room. That way, Lucy wouldn't have to wake up on Christmas morning by herself.

Anna hadn't put it quite that way, but Lucy knew that's what she'd meant.

"Not sure," Lucy made herself say. "You and Kyle should take some alone time. You won't have that much longer." She shot a pointed look at Anna's belly.

"We've had alone time every day since you moved out and Ray got married," Anna reminded her. "It's Christmas. It's about family."

"Being a third wheel isn't going to fill me with Christmas joy," Lucy all but snapped. "I'll be there for the dinner at Ray and Drew's."

Anna went silent, and Lucy moved her gaze to the computer screen, unable to meet Anna's eyes.

When Anna spoke again, her voice had gentled. "Why don't you invite Hal Jenkins to join us at the B&B?"

Lucy jerked her head up, her heart pounding in her sudden confusion. "Hal? What? Why would I?" She heard herself stammer, felt her face flame.

"I don't think he has family in town," Anna said, as though her suggestion had been perfectly reasonable. "Maybe he's alone too."

"Maybe. I don't know. Haven't talked to him in a while." Lucy groped for excuses. "He's been busy. You know, running people's ranches for them. Being a rodeo clown."

Anna rested a hip on Lucy's desk. "Did something happen between you two?"

"No." Lucy's answer was adamant. "Nothing has happened. Nothing at all." Tears stung her eyes. "Like I said, he's busy."

"Mmm." Anna's wise stare unnerved her. "What I'm thinking is that you're both staying incredibly busy so you won't have to face the fact that you like each other."

"Hal is a great guy," Lucy babbled. "But I'm not ... I don't know ... *me* anymore. I don't know what I want. Or what he wants. If anything at all. I might not even stay in Riverbend. There's a whole world out there ..."

She broke off, biting the inside of her cheek to keep from crying. Everyone, including Anna, was being so *nice* to her. Because they knew Lucy had lost everything and had come home to hide. All the sympathy was getting on her nerves.

"You can't know what Hal wants unless you ask him.

Avoiding him doesn't help." Anna stood. "Tell you what, I won't push you about him. It's your life, and it's his life, and not really my business. But the offer stands. Hal's a good friend of Ray's, and Ray would love to see him." Anna reached over and shut off Lucy's monitor. "Right now, though, I'm famished. This guy is always seriously hungry." She ran a hand over her baby bump, sudden love flooding her eyes. "Grace is the only one in town who has vegan Christmas treats, and I'm going to fill up on them. And I'm locking the door, so you need to leave."

Lucy heaved a sigh. "All right, all right. I guess I need to quit the pity party." She closed down the rest of her computer and grabbed her purse. "But no more talk about Hal. Just ... no."

"Deal," Anna said. She swung away to turn off the lights.

Hal had been one of the few who'd understood Lucy's plight when she'd suddenly returned to Riverbend. He hadn't gushed sympathy at her or asked if she wanted to talk about it. He only sat with her in silence when he saw her at the bar or when they bumped into each other at the diner. Once, at the opening of Drew's B&B, Hal had kissed her.

Lucy hadn't recovered from that yet. Hal had backed off afterward, probably afraid Lucy was still too hung up on her old life to start a new relationship.

Hal could be right. Anna could be right too, but Lucy knew she had to work through things herself. Her heartbreak had been sudden, unexpected, and shocking, and she had no idea what she was thinking or feeling anymore.

Nothing she'd get over in the few weeks everyone had seemed to hope it would take.

Lucy snatched up her coat and followed Anna out, pausing to lock up while Anna made for her truck. True, downing as many Christmas cookies and pastries as they could at her sister's bakery beat sitting in a lonely office and pretending to work.

Grace made the best cookies ever. At least coming home to Riverbend had given Lucy that.

Olivia enjoyed a brisk ride on Buster across Campbell lands to the river that afternoon, after the meeting with her sons and Carew, the cold December air bracing.

On her return, she skirted the land Dale had sold, knowing in her mind exactly where the line lay in correspondence to Carew's map. She'd held Buster to the side of the ranch she still owned, unable to put even one hoofstep over the line.

"Damn you, Dale Campbell," she said to the wind.

Buster flicked his ears to her, waiting for voice commands. Olivia patted him.

"Never mind, old guy. I'm mad at your grandfather, is all."

Buster snorted, as if he understood.

"I loved Dale," Olivia continued. "Loved him to pieces." That had been true enough, and she still loved him with great intensity.

Olivia found something refreshing about spewing her frustrations to a horse in the middle of nowhere. The ranch was quiet, and her breath fogged in the air.

"I know we never used this patch much," she continued. "But it was *ours*. I adored Dale, but he could be so pigheaded. So sure he was right. I just know he thought he'd make the money back in no time and rebuy the land." Olivia's voice grew somber. "And then he had to leave us."

A lonely road, a random accident, and Dale's life had been over.

Olivia sighed. She'd buried the grief and pain of that night deep, fearing that if she went to pieces some misguided person at River County's family services would take away her boys. She'd have died herself if that happened. Adam, Grant, Tyler, Ross—they'd been her life.

For them, she'd held it together. She'd poured her love into them, and into Circle C. For them, Olivia had suppressed her own hurt and loneliness. She'd opened the ranch to other boys and girls in need, so they wouldn't have to be alone either.

Now, Olivia was content, at least most of the time. Her sons had surpassed her wildest hopes, and her daughters-in-law filled the space of the daughters she'd never had. Her grandchildren were simply beautiful.

But out here, with only Buster for company, she admitted she was lonely.

This deceit by Dale had dredged up all kinds of memories, both sweet and sour. Everyone in town had claimed Dale had been tamed by the gentle-natured Olivia, but in reality, Olivia had been bowled over by him. Tall, handsome, blue-eyed Dale had been charming, exciting, and incredibly sexy. They hadn't been able to keep their hands off each other—there was a reason Olivia had been so often pregnant.

Olivia had believed she and Dale had become the perfect partners. But Dale had always kept a part of himself away from everyone, one that proclaimed he had to fix everything without help, one that refused to admit he needed assistance.

"I couldn't have done anything about the debts," Olivia told Buster. "But we might have made the decisions *together*."

Buster's answering huff told her he agreed, and Olivia patted him again. Buster might be a pain in the butt to her sons, but he was a great horse and a good listener.

Olivia put Buster into a swift trot, ceasing her conversation to enjoy the ride. About a half mile from the barn, she eased him back to a walk, letting him cool down before she dismounted at the hitching posts outside the barn.

None of the ranch hands rushed forward to take Buster's reins or remove the saddle she immediately uncinched. They knew from experience that Olivia liked to rub down the horses herself.

Olivia pulled the heavy saddle from Buster's back and carried it to the tack room, returning with halter, curry comb, and brush. She exchanged the bridle for the halter and started circling the curry comb over Buster's bay coat.

After a time, bootsteps crunched toward her. Olivia didn't look up, assuming it would be Bill, the oldest ranch hand who usually couldn't help but make sure Olivia didn't need anything.

"All I hear is what a shit Buster is," Sam said to her. "And here you are, walking behind him and all around him, and he doesn't move an inch."

Olivia suppressed her start of gladness and gave Buster's coat a swipe with the dandy brush. The horse half-closed his eyes in enjoyment. "We understand each other, is all."

"Looks like it," Sam remarked as Buster sighed and canted his weight to one hip.

Olivia rubbed the brushes together to clear them of excess hair, then dropped them into the grooming box and faced Sam.

"I'm glad you're here," Olivia said to him in sincerity. "I want you to tell me the truth—what is the real reason you came back to Riverbend?"

CHAPTER EIGHT

Sam jerked his attention from Buster—a horse notorious for the surreptitious kick—and found Olivia's blue eyes skewering him.

She was a beautiful lady, tough without being hard, her body honed from her years of riding, not to mention chasing after her sons. Olivia regarded him with perceptiveness as she waited for him to answer.

"I think maybe you guessed why," Sam said.

"I don't like guessing." Olivia's voice was steady. "You're living near your brother in San Antonio, in a nice house, I heard. I also heard you and Charlie pretty much live at every fishing hole around."

"True." Sam leaned an elbow on the empty hitching bar next to Buster's. "But you can only fish so often. And San Antonio is damned hot most of the time. Riverbend has cooler breezes, more trees."

"You came back for trees?"

Olivia sounded irritated. She'd been angry since Sam

had showed up at the diner to break the news about Vince owning half her ranch. The one person he hadn't wanted mad at him he'd immediately upset.

"Shit." Sam removed his hat and let it drop to the ground. Buster, seriously out of character, only glanced at it. "You know damn well why I came back, Olivia. I came back for you."

Olivia's only response was the lift of her chest with her breath. She'd taken off her hat to groom Buster and the breeze stirred her hair, the sun making her eyes sparkle. Or maybe they glistened with tears?

"Why did you leave in the first place?" she asked, voice quiet. "I've always been right here."

Sam balled one fist. "Because I didn't know what you'd do if I turned up on your doorstep. We've been friends for so long ..."

"And you thought I wouldn't want more?" Her question held tension.

Sam's throat tightened. "How could I know what you wanted, Livie? You never said a word to me. You were there for me when Caro died, but then you backed way off."

"Giving you time to heal, or at least to grieve." Pain shadowed Olivia's face. "I don't know if we ever heal."

"Nope." Sam knew that for a fact. "But we can keep living."

Olivia huffed a laugh and raked fingers through her hair. "Well, I certainly did that."

"No, you didn't," Sam returned. "For a long time, you were just surviving."

He remembered the wooden way Olivia had moved

after Dale's death, even when she'd been surrounded by her sons, marching them through town, taking them for haircuts or to buy clothes for school, or helping them unload their horses for junior rodeo competitions at the Fall Festival.

Olivia studied the hills she'd just ridden across. "You might have a point."

"I don't think you started living again until after Faith came along," Sam stated. "I remember you telling me how Carter walked into the house holding a tiny baby like it might explode in his hands. You laughed about it, and I saw the light come back into your eyes."

Olivia returned her gaze, which had softened, to Sam. "Faith is a sweet girl. I saw her change Carter in a way I never could."

"So, you'll understand when I tell you I was just surviving when I left Riverbend three years ago," Sam concluded. "I needed to go. To sit beside a lake with my brother and think about things."

"And drink beer and catch fish."

Sam let his face crease in a brief grin. "That too. We'd get some good striped bass to take home."

"There's even better fishing around Riverbend," Olivia said, tone casual. Her rigidness had eased. "I'm thinking that lured you back as well?"

Sam lost his amusement. "No, Olivia." He closed the distance between them. "If you'll stop talking about fishing for just one second ..."

"I like to fish." Her voice went soft. "Good angling up at the bend."

Sam stepped even closer. "We should go then."

Olivia never moved, her gaze flicking from his eyes to his lips. "We should. Tomorrow?"

"I'll get my gear." Sam touched the curve of her cheek. "For right now ..."

He trailed off and did what he'd been dreaming of for the last three years.

Sam leaned to Olivia and kissed her on the mouth.

It was a sweet kiss, full of sunshine and warmth, with a touch of need. Sam's loneliness, which had beaten at him for a long time now, started to whimper and fade.

The breeze touched them with winter chill. Sam slid his arms around Olivia, the beautiful, laughing girl he'd known since his youth, whose presence and comfort had taken him through the worst pain imaginable.

She was here with him, a pillar of warmth as well as a welcoming and soft woman. Her responding kiss opened things inside him Sam thought closed. Need, which he'd assumed long gone, rose with heat.

Fulfilling need would have to come later. For now, the taste of Olivia's lips, her tongue against his, her fingers gripping his shoulders—this was heaven. This was *right*.

Buster snorted his opinion, but Olivia drew Sam closer, renewing the kiss. Sam smiled as they came together, tangled things in his life beginning to straighten and smooth.

"OH, HELL NO."

Grant Campbell stopped short as he charged out of the office, intent on the stables to begin training, and the words jerked from his mouth. Adam, coming out behind him, almost slammed into his back.

"What?" Adam demanded. Grant felt Adam push past him with impatience and then his brother also rocked to a halt. "Well, shit."

Grant wasn't certain what he felt as he gazed past the training arena to the corner of the barn where Buster stood like a lump, watching Olivia kissing Sam Farrell.

The brothers stared in shock for a long moment before Adam chuckled. "It's about damned time."

"Seriously?" Grant asked in amazement. "You saw this coming?"

"You didn't?" Adam shook his head and started for the corral where two newer horses awaited them to begin lunge-line work. "Sam's had a thing for mom for a while now, didn't you realize that? And she for him. Why do you think he quit town for so long?"

Sam had been like part of the furniture when Grant had been growing up. Around a lot, but Grand had thought of him as just a friend of their dad's, and then Christina's caring uncle.

"Huh." Grant dialed back his surprise, realizing Adam was right. Mom and Sam had known each other forever, and it was natural that they'd sought each other out. They needed each other, Grant recognized, but the difference in their relationship was going to take some adjustment.

"You know that if they get married, Sam will be both

our stepdad and uncle-in-law," Grant pointed out. "That's just weird."

Adam laughed, one of the hearty laughs he'd found again since he'd gotten back with Bailey. "It's a hazard of living in a small town. Suck it up."

"I'm not calling him Dad," Grant said darkly. "I'll stick with Uncle Sam."

"Don't get ahead of yourself," Adam told him. "They're just kissing." He paused. "And kissing. Think they're going to run out of air?"

Grant shielded his face as he strode toward the corral. "Let's move along. Nothing to see here."

Adam laughed again as he followed his brother, Grant's heart lightening as he went.

If Sam could erase the last of the shadows in his mother's eyes, Grant would give the man a hug and call him anything Sam wanted him to.

BEING WITH SAM WAS RELAXING, OLIVIA DECIDED. Well, not relaxing exactly. The man kissed like fire. He'd proved that without doubt at the barn yesterday.

Peaceful might be a better word. On the morning two days before Christmas, they stood side by side at Olivia's favorite fishing spot at the river bottom, lines in the water. Their only conversation so far had pertained to fishing. There wasn't much talking at all, which was fine with Olivia.

Adam and Grant had seen her and Sam together

yesterday. While neither of her sons had said a word to her, they'd avoided looking at her the rest of the evening, except to shoot her grins when they thought she didn't see them.

They'd kept it to themselves, though—she'd known that from the obliviousness of Carter and Tyler—and Ross hadn't visited yesterday at all.

Ah, well. There would be time enough to face the family with this new relationship.

Whatever it was. Two people sharing days? Or something more permanent? And was Olivia ready for that?

One thing she loved about Sam was that he didn't push. He stood next to her today, solid in his fleece-lined coat, hat firmly in place, and simply fished. Sam's arms worked as he cast his line, his jaw firm, eyes clear as he gazed over the water.

The fish were biting on this cold day, enough clouds rolling in to shield the direct sun, and soon the pair had a string of bass to tote home.

"Grace will do wonders with these." Olivia admired the sleek fish. "But she'll want them cleaned."

"I'll do that," Sam said without rancor. "Charlie's Loretta never lets us in the house until the fish are nice filets or steaks."

Olivia sent him a smile then the two packed up. They'd walked the few miles from the ranch, and Sam laid the fish on ice in a cooler for the walk home.

"You'll get it back," Sam said as they climbed from the riverbank to flatter land above. They took a moment to gaze over the rolling meadows that made up Circle C. "This afternoon, it will be resolved. I know it. Karen says ..."

"Let's not talk about it," Olivia interrupted quickly. She trudged a few steps, welcoming the chill wind. "I don't want it to be a thing between us. The question of the land will work out, somehow, but I want us to be *us*."

Sam's brows went up. "Okay, but I'm ..."

"Please." Olivia didn't want the stress of the past swooping in to ruin this moment, this wonderful afternoon.

Sam regarded her in surprise then shrugged. "I know I didn't make you happy barging in on your business. I hate that the first thing I did when I saw you again was piss you off."

"I wasn't mad at *you*," Olivia assured him. She hadn't been. Nick Carew, Vince Morgan, and her husband Dale had been the targets of her wrath. "I'm grateful to you, actually."

She closed her mouth, not wanting to rehash what she'd been going through. Sam had set up a meeting with Karen and Vince for tomorrow, and Olivia had agreed to attend. Karen had something up her sleeve, and Sam did too, by his expression, but at the moment, Olivia wanted nothing but the wind and scent of winter grasslands, and Sam.

Sam drew close to her, his large hand finding hers. They walked home in silence, Sam's warmth cutting the cold breeze and winding new happiness through Olivia's heart.

WHEN SAM ENTERED THE CONFERENCE ROOM AT THE bank building the next morning, he was happy to see that

Vince had actually showed up. Vince wore a neutral expression, so there was no telling what he might pull, but at least he was there.

Olivia, who had paused to greet Karen in the hall, halted in surprise as she followed Sam in.

"Callie?" She addressed Callie Jones-Campbell, Ross's wife, who turned from the window with her warm smile. "What are you doing here, honey?"

"It's all part of the meeting," Sam said before Callie could answer. "We need to wait for Karen."

Sam eyeballed Vince, silently warning him to keep his mouth shut. Vince shrugged and turned his gaze studiously to a painting of the river surrounded by spring wildflowers.

Olivia frowned, not pleased she wasn't in the loop. Sam had asked Karen not to reveal the plan until they could get everyone in a room together. With Callie there—the youngest daughter of the family Vince was in awe of— things had a better chance of going Olivia's way.

No Campbell brothers were allowed to attend this meeting. Sam had explained that to Adam, who'd understood, even if he wasn't thrilled. This might go badly if Sam filled the room with five angry Campbells ready to stomp on Vince if he said the wrong thing. Vince held all the cards in this situation, and the man knew it.

Callie gave Olivia a hug, which Olivia returned, nonplussed. The two women parted, and Callie took her seat, Olivia sinking down next to her.

"Can someone please tell me what is going on?" Olivia asked the question with stiff politeness, but Sam heard the firmness behind her words. She didn't like to be messed around.

Karen stalked in and closed the door, the latch making a loud click. She carried a stack of folders, exactly five, and moved around the table, carefully placing one each in front of Olivia, Callie, Vince, and Sam, keeping one for herself.

"Sam approached me earlier this week with an interesting proposition," Karen said, her tone smooth. "Not that kind, Mr. Morgan."

She sent Vince's chuckle a severe frown. Karen had the reputation of being a man-chaser, but inside a conference room, she was nothing but business.

"What kind?" Olivia asked as she opened the folder. She read the first sheet and her eyes widened.

"Sam?" Karen turned to him, her smile encouraging.

Sam cleared his throat. He didn't like the spotlight, but he was grateful Karen had agreed to let him make the announcement to Olivia himself.

"My idea is this. Callie doesn't renew the lease next year for her horse rehab facility on Vince's ranch. Vince donates his half of Circle C Ranch to her organization, and Callie moves the rehab place there. Vince gets a hefty tax break for giving a large piece of property to a nonprofit, and he also gets to rent out his old ranch to someone else. Everyone in Riverbend thinks Vince is a great guy, and Circle C stays in the family."

CHAPTER NINE

Sam waited in trepidation as Olivia swiftly leafed through pages of the agreement Karen had put together. When Olivia raised her head, her eyes were shining but held wariness.

"You agreed to this, Vince?" she asked.

Vince shrugged, reddening. "Sam drives a hard bargain. So does Karen." He sighed. "I wasn't doing anything with that land anyway."

Olivia peered at Sam, as though waiting for more explanation, but he'd said his piece, and had nothing to add. The chat Karen had arranged with Vince and Sam about this plan two nights ago had been pointed. Karen had supplied the business details and the ice-cold smile.

"You are willing to accept this, Callie?" Olivia asked.

"Oh, yes," Callie answered. "Nicole and I were ecstatic when Karen called us. If we have our own place, we'll be able to do so much more."

Sam glanced at Vince to see how he responded to

Callie's enthusiasm. Vince had been adamant he'd not work with Campbells, but he'd readily agreed to make a deal with Callie Jones. Now Vince's gaze went to Olivia, his face still.

In that moment, Sam saw clearly why Vince had bought the land all those years ago and hadn't asked for a penny for its use, and why he hadn't wanted Sam or the Campbell brothers to purchase it back.

Vince was in love with Olivia. Probably had been for a long time. Sam guessed Vince had been thrilled to see Dale having to beg Carew for help. Vince must have been happy, knowing *his* actions had kept Olivia out of a bind. Then he'd quietly let her use the land all these years without a word, her silent benefactor.

If Dale hadn't been killed, Vince likely would have charged him a fortune to lease the acreage or maybe offered to sell it back to him at an exorbitant price. Vince had exercised his form of kindness only to help Olivia.

"What about you, Vince?" Karen prompted. "Are you willing to sign?"

Vince dragged his gaze from Olivia and nodded, if reluctantly. "I'm okay with that. But the land is for *Callie*, not any of the Campbell boys."

"I understand." Olivia's tone went flinty. Vince wouldn't win any points with her for disparaging her sons, but he must resent the fact that Dale had sired such fine young men.

Olivia looked away from Vince, pausing at Sam before she returned to study the paperwork. The glance, as brief as it was, heated Sam all the way through.

Karen produced pens and laid them in front of Callie and Vince. "Shall we?"

Callie eagerly scribbled her name in the places Karen indicated, her pen loud in the stillness. Vince, less enthusiastically, signed away his ownership.

A young woman who worked for the bank had slipped in and now sat at the end of the table, her notary stamp ready, to make sure the documents were official.

"Congratulations, Callie," Karen said once the signing, stamping, initialing, and sealing were done. She shook Callie's hand. "And Vince. Riverbend will sing your praises."

"Yeah, well." Vince rose. Sam got up as well, as did Olivia.

"Thank you, Vince," Olivia said. She reached for Vince's hand and clasped it in a businesslike grip. "I appreciate it, and I won't forget it."

Vince turned a shade of red that matched the scarlet wildflowers in the painting. "Sure thing." He slowly released Olivia and sent Sam a curt nod. "Farrell."

With another nod to Callie, Vince took himself out of the conference room. His tread in the hall was heavy.

Callie enfolded Olivia in an excited embrace. "I can't wait to start the move," she said as they parted. "We need to decide how the stables should to be built and how to arrange the facilities, and well, everything." She waved her hands in the air. "Plus being at Circle C all the time will be fantastic. Ross will be so happy."

"So will I, sweetie," Olivia said with sincerity. She turned to Karen, putting on a determined expression.

"While we're here, I want to continue with my plan to gift the ranch to my sons, at least the part of it I actually own."

Sam expected Callie to break in, saying Ross wouldn't hear of it, or some such, but Callie remained silent, calm, and confident.

Karen competently slid signed papers back into their folders. "You've been preempted," she said. "Your sons and their wives have already started the process of buying the land from you. Congratulations, Ms. Campbell. You will be a very rich woman."

Olivia gaped at her, then her lips firmed. "Not if I won't let them. I want to *give* them that land, free and clear."

"If you'll pardon me," Karen interrupted. "It's much more sensible this way. There will be a record of the property's current worth if you sell it for its full value. Your sons have plenty of money and don't need a mortgage—this will be a cash sale. If you're worried about Ross on his county sheriff's salary, he's paying what he can afford and no more. I'd take their offer, Olivia."

"I agree," Sam said. He knew Olivia wasn't pleased, but Sam faced her without flinching. "You worked your ass off your whole life, Livie. Now it's your turn to enjoy yourself. Take the money, go anywhere in the world you want. Even if where you want to be is right here in Riverbend."

"What will you do, Sam?" Olivia asked, her eyes sharp. "Stay in Riverbend? Or run off to fish in San Antonio again?"

Sam stepped closer to her, taking her hands. Her skin was smooth and soft, though he felt her fingers tremble.

"Wherever you decide to go, Liv, that's where I'll be too. If you want me to be."

Olivia's face lost its stiffness as her grip on his hands tightened. Sam noted Karen, Callie, and the notary watching the little scene with interest.

Aware of their scrutiny, Olivia sent him the barest nod. "We'll talk about it," she said softly. "Thank you, Sam." Her smile was warm, genuine.

She released him and walked out of the room, her footfalls quiet.

―――

Christmas morning at Circle C Ranch began early. Carter entered the living room of the suite he and Grace lived in on one end of the ranch house before anyone else was up. He turned on a small lamp in the dark room, quietly, so as not to wake his daughter and son.

He studied the space he'd enlarged after he and Grace had married, making room for their growing family. They'd added another bedroom and bathroom to the suite he and Faith had occupied for years, plus a small kitchen where Grace could cook just for Carter and her children. The suite had become another house within the house.

A small Christmas tree stood in the corner. The tree had been decorated by Faith and Grace, with small Zach "helping"—which meant nearly knocking over the entire tree, breaking anything that could be broken, and putting whatever he could reach into his mouth.

Carter liked the now lopsided tree hung with decorations Faith had made herself, especially the ones with big glittery letters that spelled out *Zach*, *Faith*, *Grace / Mom*, and *Dad*. Wrapped gifts lay tumbled under the tree, waiting for impatient fingers.

A mug of coffee was shoved into his hands. The next moment, Grace warmed Carter's side, her oversized robe warm and soft.

"I can't believe we're awake before they are," she whispered. "This is lucky."

"I made sure." Carter had trained himself over the years to wake up any time he needed to. "But yeah, luck helped."

"Either that or they're exhausted."

Christmas Eve had been a flurry of preparations, last minute shopping, gift wrapping, baking, and prepping for today's feast in the main house.

"Bit of both," Carter said.

He slipped his arm around Grace and took a sip of coffee, which was rich and hot, just how he liked it. Grace cuddled into his side, the robe filled with her sweet curves. Just how he liked *her*.

Lucky, Grace had said. Yes, Carter was damned lucky. First, that Faith was his kid. She'd taught Carter how to love like no other. Next, that Grace sat here against him, a smile on her face as she held her own cup of coffee, her hair tickling his chin. When Grace Malory had announced she loved him, Carter's whole world had changed.

He kissed the top of her head. Last night, right after midnight, Carter had watched Grace tiredly shed her clothes before she'd crawled into their bed and snuggled down with him. Carter had assumed she'd drop off to sleep after all the work she'd been doing, but she'd sent him a sly glance as she'd turned off the lamp, slid over him, and kissed him deeply.

Carter had made swift love to her then they'd fallen asleep, spooned together, neither moving until Carter had pried himself out of bed a few minutes ago.

This quiet time now was almost as good as their frenzied lovemaking last night. A peace between them, no talking necessary.

A wailing cry broke the silence. Grace's smile turned wry as she popped to her feet. "I knew it wouldn't take long."

Carter stood. "You stay. I'll go."

Grace plopped back down. "Won't say no."

Carter chuckled as he made for the door to Zach's room. Another door opened, and Faith trotted out in her pajamas, hair tousled, her eyes barely open.

"Did I miss it?"

"Christmas?" Carter checked his stride to go to Faith and hug her. "Just getting started. Morning, angel."

He kissed her cheek, and Faith returned the kiss. "Morning, Dad. Morning, Grace." Her voice gained strength as her sleepiness fled. "Morning, Zach," she called as Zach hollered again. The boy sure knew how to get attention.

"Merry Christmas, Faith." Grace opened her arms, and Faith zinged to her, hopping up on the sofa and into Grace's embrace.

Carter entered Zach's room, moving to the boy who sat

up in his crib, mouth open in a roar. Carter lifted him, and Zach's cries cut off like he'd thrown a switch. He wrapped his hands around Carter's neck and gave his father a wet kiss on the cheek.

"Merry Christmas, Zach," Carter said softly.

He carried the little miracle out to the living room, Zach reaching for Grace as soon as Carter sat down again. Carter lifted the bouncing Faith onto his lap, kissing the top of her head as he basked in his family, his home.

Grace was right. He sure was damn lucky.

A LITTLE WAY UP THE ROAD FROM CIRCLE C A LONG, low house held similar early morning activity.

Three-year-old Dale burst from his bedroom with a drawn-out shriek of delight and charged into the living room. Bailey watched him do a dive worthy of a baseball star sliding for home, ending up at the stack of presents under the tree.

"Which one's mine? Which one's mine?" Dale bellowed.

Adam, devastating in shorts, T-shirt, and bare feet joined Dale at the tree, thumping down, cross-legged, next to his son.

"A whole bunch are yours," Adam said. "Let's sort these out."

Bailey, with much-needed coffee, seated herself on the edge of the sofa and watched Adam take charge.

Morning sunlight brushed the scars on her husband's

face. They'd faded from the angry red they'd been soon after his accident but were still there. She'd heard some people say they'd ruined his once handsome looks, but Bailey didn't agree. Adam Campbell had always been the most gorgeous man she knew, and she hadn't changed that opinion.

No matter what had happened, Adam was still *him*. The stunt-riding hunk who'd tried to hide his embarrassment as he'd asked for Bailey's help so he could graduate, the movie stuntman turned famous, and the broken man who'd returned home to heal were Adam, and only Adam.

Bailey loved him hard.

She observed Adam and Dale sitting side-by-side, the little boy already showing his father's set of head, stubborn firmness of jaw, and flash of sunny grin.

Adam turned to her. "And this one's for Bailey."

Dale snatched a glittery box from Adam, rolled to his feet, and marched it her. "It's for you, Mom. Open it. Open it."

Bailey tore through the wrapping with enough fervor for Dale's satisfaction and pulled out a small box. She lifted its lid, her breath catching as she saw what was inside.

It was a photograph of Adam and Bailey holding Dale between them that Ross had snapped sometime this past year at a family do. Adam had set the photo into an oval frame. Lying next to it in the box was a locket suspended from a gold chain that held a picture of Adam on one side and Dale on the other.

"Oh, they're beautiful." Bailey slid from the couch,

holding the locket chain around her neck. "Put this on me. I want to wear it for Christmas."

Adam moved to her, his smile warming her to her toes. Heating her even more was Adam's fingers gentle on the back of her neck as he fastened the chain.

Adam turned her around, hands in hers. "Dale helped me pick it out."

"Thank you." Bailey blinked back tears. "You two are the sweetest guys in the world."

"We do our best." Adam's grin made her heart thump.

Bailey rose on tiptoes and kissed Adam's parted lips. He responded with fire, his arms going around her to pull her close.

A boulder ran into Bailey's legs, small arms clutching her and Adam both. "Ewww," Dale said. "Kissy face."

Laughing, Adam hoisted Dale into his arms, welcoming him into their embrace. Bailey flushed with happiness, kissing Dale's cheek.

Adam's searing gaze sent Bailey a message of love and a promise of heat to come before he carried Dale back to the tree and the waiting wealth of presents.

―――

CHRISTINA CAMPBELL WELCOMED GRANT INTO HER AS he woke her at dawn. She smothered her groans as they came together, he rocking into her with fire. Grant always made love like a man starving, and Christina responded in kind.

They had to keep their cries quiet these days, and

Christina sent hers in a blanket crammed to her mouth. She released a long sigh which turned into laughter as Grant collapsed on top of her.

"Merry Christmas," she whispered.

"Oh, yeah." Grant said with feeling. "Merry Christmas to you too, baby."

Christina wound down into the joy that was Grant. She couldn't believe that they'd once pushed each other away, but now they understood each other better than they had before. The bond they'd forged had only grown stronger.

Christina drifted back to sleep, she and Grant snuggling into blankets against the winter cold. Not for long. The door banged open, and Emma landed hard in the middle of the bed.

"Wake up, wake up, wake up!" Emma climbed to her feet and jumped up and down on the mattress until Grant, tangled in blankets, caught her around the waist.

"Enough of that, little monster."

Emma threw her arms around Grant then almost instantly wriggled out of his grasp. "It's Christmas, it's Christmas!"

"Yeah, it is." Grant lifted Emma from the bed, setting her on her feet. "You go on out there. Mom and I are right behind you."

Emma charged out as energetically as she'd charged in, her arms high, hands in fists. Christina laughed—it was so good simply to laugh with delight at her daughter.

Grant got himself out of bed, pulling pajamas over his

naked body. Christina lingered, taking time to admire him, her handsome cowboy, all the way down.

Then she heaved herself up, throwing on a top and sweatpants, and took Grant's hand to join Emma, who was romping around the tree. Christina laughed again, her heart light, her world exactly as it should be.

———

A FEW HOURS LATER, TYLER HOISTED BABY SARAH IN his arms as Jess herded twelve-year-old Dominic out of the house. Dominic had a giant cardboard box in his arms that he struggled to heft.

"You can play with all that later, Dominic," Jess told him. Her son had piled all his Christmas gifts into the box, determined to lug them with him.

"I want to show Faith what I got."

Jess hid a pang as she recalled the many years she'd only been able to give Dominic a few meager gifts at Christmas. Now Tyler showered him with them. When Jess protested that Tyler was buying too much, the generous Tyler brushed it aside.

"You're only a kid for a little while," Tyler had told her. "When I was his age, we had nothing. Mom did her best, but we had to make do with not much. It's fun to watch Dominic enjoy all the stuff."

One part of the "stuff" this year was a small four-wheel off-road vehicle, which fortunately Dominic didn't try to drag with him today.

"We can invite Faith over later, and you can show her everything then," Jess promised.

Dominic thought this through, then shrugged, finding the suggestion reasonable. "Okay." He trotted back inside the house she and Tyler had built not far from the ranch, returning with only a shoebox-sized wrapped present plus a brand-new phone he'd already loaded his favorite tunes onto. "She'll think this is cool."

Faith was going on thirteen, still riding and loving her cowboy gear, but also starting to like earrings and pretty clothes. Jess hoped Faith wouldn't leave Dominic behind as she grew up, but that remained to be seen. Faith was a sunny-natured girl, and Jess doubted she'd deliberately hurt her old friends as she changed into a young woman.

"What did you get her?" Tyler asked him.

Dominic slid the phone into his back pocket and patted the gift. "It's a box she can keep her curry combs and stuff in. I decorated it with horse pictures and also motorcycle stuff."

Tyler sent Jess a wink that made her toes curl inside her boots. "Trying to make her a biker like your mom?" Tyler asked.

"Faith likes motorcycles. When we get older, we can ride together."

Tyler exchanged another glance with Jess. Dominic, oblivious to their shared speculation, opened Tyler's pickup and slid into his place in the back seat.

"He's got it all mapped out," Tyler told Jess in a low voice. Sarah, in a knit hat against the wind, cooed at the sound of her father's words.

"We'll see what happens," Jess said. She wasn't going to puncture Dominic's romantic dreams. She knew from experience that the world tried to do that too often.

Tyler wrapped his arm around Jess. "I think it will work out. It did for us. Made me believe in hope again."

"Me too," Jess said softly.

She leaned against him, her strong cowboy who knew how to support her weaker side, the love in her heart flaring. Sarah grinned a watery smile, happy that her mom and dad were so close.

"Come on, Mom," Dominic called to her. "We'll never get there."

Jess laughed. She kissed Tyler on the mouth, tasting his heat, then kissed Sarah lightly on the forehead. She made for the pickup, where her son waited impatiently to bestow Christmas cheer on the family he'd so readily bonded with.

AT THE MALORY RANCH ON THE OTHER SIDE OF TOWN, Lucy's breakfast with Kyle and Anna was interrupted by Anna's cell phone buzzing.

"It's Callie," Anna said as she studied the phone's screen. She leapt up from the table, hurrying into the living room with enviable agility so she could ask in concern, "What's up?"

Lucy smiled to herself as she watched Kyle gaze longingly after his wife, his eyes full of love. It was so sweet.

Anna had finally talked Lucy into spending the night of Christmas Eve in her old room at the ranch. That way,

Anna had said, Lucy could have Christmas morning breakfast and gifts with her and Kyle before they headed to Ray and Drew's afternoon feast.

Lucy admitted it was nice to come downstairs to the sunny kitchen, where both Kyle and Anna had cooked up a mess of eggs and pancakes—vegetarian versions of everything for Anna. Lucy didn't mind tucking into both traditional pancakes and those made with coconut milk and oil, slathering all with maple syrup. Now that she didn't have a boyfriend who expected a severely thin woman on his arm, Lucy had begun to enjoy eating hearty breakfasts once more.

Anna glided back into the kitchen. "I have to go," she said. "Callie says one of the horses is down with colic." She huffed a laugh. "Horses don't take Christmas off."

Even as she spoke, she was gathering up her emergency vet box she kept for calls like these. As ranchers, both Lucy and Kyle knew horse emergencies were urgent and couldn't be ignored.

"I'll come with you," Kyle said, already on his feet to assist.

"No way." Anna swung from him, reaching for her puffy jacket, Christmas Day having dawned cold. "You need to babysit your chili so it will be ready to go to Ray's."

"Ray can do without it," Kyle answered. He reached for his jacket as well, but Anna pulled his arm back.

"Seriously, sweetie, I'm a big girl," Anna said. "You don't need to accompany me to every call. I've been doing this on my own for years."

"Not preggers you haven't." Kyle scowled. "You're

running around dangerous animals. A colicky horse can kick or even roll on you."

Lucy knew Kyle had a point, but Anna put on her stubborn face. "The animals I treat seem to understand I'm pregnant. They're gentle."

Kyle continued to glower, his worry evident. Lucy stepped in. "I'll go with you, Anna. I'm supposed to be your assistant. So, I'll assist."

Anna nodded without hesitation. "I can't say I won't welcome the help. But *you* stay home." She pointed a slim finger at Kyle. "You'll only hover."

She softened to give Kyle a kiss, one that turned lingering. Lucy averted her gaze, unable to stop a grin. She liked seeing her big brother put in his place, but also like seeing him so much in love.

Anna ended the kiss, slid from Kyle's embrace, and headed for the door.

Thank you, Kyle mouthed at Lucy, and Lucy gave him a thumbs-up before snatching up the emergency kit and following Anna out.

It was nice stepping out into the brisk morning air, Lucy decided as she followed Anna to her small pickup. While she'd been enjoying Christmas breakfast, to her surprise, her restlessness made her leap at the chance to drive out to the rehab ranch.

"He's so protective," Anna growled. She started the truck once they were settled and pulled away from the house, waving at Kyle who'd come onto the porch to watch them go.

"Tell me about it," Lucy said. "I grew up with him. But it means he loves you."

Anna's expression lightened. "I suppose that's true."

"Please don't go on about how much you love him too." Lucy grimaced. "He's my brother."

Anna laughed, and they headed down the deserted road toward the rehab ranch. The sky was empty of clouds, but the air was icy, the sun barely warming it. Sunlight glittered on the fences they passed, splinters of frost like diamonds.

Frost also coated the roofs of the house, trailer, and barns at the Morgan ranch, which was busy this morning. As Anna said, horses didn't take days off. Callie's rehab organization had rescued nearly twenty equines, and now men and women moved through the barn and mare pens, dispensing hay or mucking out stalls.

Anna parked and calmly exited the car, this just another call for her. Lucy slid out and lifted the emergency box.

"Hey, Dr. Anna," the exuberant tones of Manny Judd floated to them. "Hi, Lucy. Merry Christmas, you guys. Horse is down here." He pointed to the open barn where Callie lingered, Ross with her. Callie waved, and they all headed that way. "Guess who I'm having Christmas dinner with?" Manny danced sideways, his boots raising dust. "The Harrisons, that's who," he finished triumphantly before either Anna or Lucy could say a word.

Manny had been going out with Tracy Harrison, Deputy Harrison's younger sister, for a bit now. Harrison must have decided Manny was all right if he'd actually invited him to Christmas dinner.

"That's great, Manny." Lucy sent him an encouraging smile. "Be sure to mind your manners, though. Remember, Tracy's brother can arrest you."

Manny's sparkle dimmed minutely. "Yeah, I remember. Trust me, I have that in mind all the time."

Lucy decided to quit teasing him. "Well, I'm sure—"

She broke off, the air suddenly leaving her throat. Anna had already hurried on to meet Callie, and Manny trotted after Anna, too impatient to listen to Lucy's advice.

A large man had emerged from the barn, blinking against the sunlight before he rested a cowboy hat on his head. He saw Lucy and stopped. Anna and the others moved past him as though he were a boulder in a stream.

"Lucy," Hal Jenkins said.

CHAPTER TEN

Hal tried to make his feet move toward Lucy, but they were mired in place. The icy mud might as well be cement.

She looked beautiful this morning in jeans, cowboy boots, and heavy jacket against the cold. The breeze tossed her dark hair, which she wore short, and sunlight made her green eyes glow.

He should have figured she'd come with Dr. Anna. Lucy was Anna's shadow now, handing her tools or holding the horses or cows while Anna injected or prodded them. Lucy was good with horses, talking to them gently, stroking a nose or neck to keep them distracted as Dr. Anna worked.

Hal cleared his throat and tried to speak again. "Hey," was all he managed.

Lucy, who'd simply stared at him while Hal stood poleaxed, answered, "Hey, yourself. What are you doing here?"

Her voice was like music. Hal could listen to it all day.

"I said, what are you doing here?" Lucy repeated the question slowly and carefully, and Hal jumped.

"Oh. Yeah. I'm helping Callie. A lot of volunteers want off for Christmas, and she needs extra hands. I wasn't doing anything else, so ..." Hal shrugged and trailed off before he babbled any more.

"Yeah, well I'm helping out Anna." Lucy hefted the box under her arm. "And Kyle, really. He worries about her."

"Natural," Hal said. "First kid and all."

Like he'd know anything about that. Hal had no children, no family. He swallowed and pushed the thoughts away.

An awkward silence descended. Hal always liked that he never had to come up with scintillating conversation for Lucy, but at the same time, he couldn't just stand here staring at her like a fool.

He flashed back to the kiss they'd shared at the grand opening of Drew's B&B. Lucy's warm lips on his, her body sweet in his arms. Her breath had touched his cheek, and Hal had grown hot, staying that way for the rest of the day.

Lucy had beat a retreat after that kiss, and they'd been stiff around each other ever since.

"So, um," Hal began.

"Hal," Lucy said at the same time. "Oh, sorry. You go ahead."

"No." Panic rose in his chest. "You first."

Both of them closed their mouths. Hal firmed his, letting no uncomfortable speech escape.

Lucy drew a breath. "All right. Ray and Drew are

having a Malory Christmas feast at the B&B. Well, family and whatever guests have booked rooms. Grace and Carter will be coming. And me. Why don't you—?" She broke off and coughed as though her mouth had suddenly gone dry. "Ray would love to see you," she croaked. "Come join us. You don't have to bring anything. There will be plenty of food, plus Kyle's making a vat of chili—"

"Yeah, okay." Hal flinched inwardly as the words tumbled out of his mouth. Why had he agreed, and so fast?

Lucy flushed, and he couldn't tell whether she was pleased or dismayed by his answer.

"Well, then." Lucy switched the toolbox from one arm to the other. "Guess I'll see you there. I have to ..." She motioned past him to the barn's entrance.

"Sure." Hal stepped aside, realizing he'd been blocking the way. Anna waited down the shadowy breezeway at the stall with the colicky horse.

"Thanks." Lucy hurried past him, her warmth brushing him.

Her relief to end the awkward conversation was evident. Easier to be with an animal than talk to a human. Hal had always found that to be true.

Lucy slanted him a smile as she went, one that sent heat straight into his heart. Hal waited until she'd joined Anna, Callie, Ross, and Manny, who were discussing the horse's symptoms, before he took himself to the mare pens to continue assisting the volunteers.

Hal wasn't certain what he felt about the upcoming Christmas feast, dread and anticipation whirling back and forth inside him. He only knew that when he was beside Lucy, the whole world suddenly became right.

―――

Karen Marvin spent Christmas morning as she'd done since her last divorce—with a luxurious sleep in, a fresh pot of Puerto Rican coffee she ordered directly from a coffee planter on that island, and her feet up on the couch. She read through the Christmas cards from friends and a few from various ex's grown children she still kept in touch with. She'd long ago decided their asshole fathers weren't their fault.

She didn't mind being alone in her nice house in White Fork, which she'd fixed up exactly as she wanted it. Better a quiet morning to herself than having to face a cheating dickhead across the breakfast table and wonder how to save her marriage.

Being alone was so much less stressful.

But kind of lonely too. Karen had listened to the Campbells talk about their big family Christmas dinner, as well as other clients listing the family members coming to see them or the places they were going to visit family and friends.

Karen hadn't made plans to spend Christmas with anyone, and a tug of wistfulness nearly spoiled her perfect cup of coffee. Not that she wanted to be in a houseful of Campbells as the brothers threw jokes at each other, the kids ran around screaming, and the wives tried to put their heads together to come up with a guy for Karen. Karen could find her own men, thank you.

She set down her cup and stared out into the yard, frost sparkling on the winter-yellow grass.

"Damn it," she said, voice ringing. "Don't be such a stupid wimp."

Her orange-striped tabby, draped over the end of the sofa, opened one green eye and gazed at Karen inquiringly.

"Not you, sweetie," Karen told him. "Me. I didn't make plans because I thought I could make them with Jack, and I know it."

Instead, Jack had told her he'd be out of town until January. Things to take care of. That might mean anything from a business deal for his lumberyard, to visiting an old or current girlfriend, or bailing a family member out of jail. Jack didn't talk much about his past or even his present life. He could have a wife and seven kiddies tucked away somewhere for all she knew.

Karen had enough connections that she could easily have him checked out. Every one of his secrets revealed, at least those that were in a record somewhere.

She hadn't wanted to. Afraid of what she'd find? Probably.

"I'm stupid and getting old." She'd be forty soon enough.

Karen sighed. No use growing morose over a guy she'd only gone out with a few times. It wasn't like she was ready to marry him—or anyone for that matter.

She lifted her cup to her lips, found the coffee cold, and grimaced. "Fresh cup. That will do the trick."

As she headed to the kitchen, the phone in the pocket of her thick plush robe buzzed. Karen fished it out, wondering who the hell would be contacting her on Christmas morning, and then stopped dead. A few droplets of cooled coffee splashed to her pristine wooden floor.

Hey Karen, the text said. *Just thinking about you. Merry Christmas.*

Jack's rare texts were always brief and to the point. Karen had learned to savor every word.

She quickly set down the cup and tapped letters for a message back, fingers shaking.

Merry Christmas to you too. See you soon.

After Karen sent the text, she mentally kicked herself. She should have waited, not let him think she was eagerly hovering over her phone for his messages.

Another text popped up almost immediately. *Yep.*

Then nothing. Karen closed her eyes and hugged the phone to her chest.

When it buzzed again, she nearly dropped it in her anxiousness to read Jack's next message. She let out a strangled laugh when she saw Drew Paresky-Malory's name on her screen instead.

Hi, Karen. If you don't have other plans today, we'd love to see you at the B&B for our Christmas gathering. We never could have done all this without you. About 1 PM?

Karen grew amused at herself for how rapidly she responded. *I'd love to. I'll be there.*

She slid her phone into the pocket, hurried to the kitchen to refill her coffee, and hummed as she made new plans for the day.

―――

"Who knew I'd love Christmas in a little town," Erica, Drew's daughter, burbled as she peeled potatoes for Drew in the kitchen. Several turkeys and a ham roasted in the kitchen's large ovens, the aroma of basted meat and stuffing filling the room. "It's like a postcard around here, one of those old-fashioned ones. We just need snow and people ice-skating on a pond."

"The ponds around here don't freeze," Ray said. He lumbered in to fetch another load of plates to set on the table, brushing a kiss to Drew's cheek as he passed. "At least not thick enough or long enough to skate on. I do not recommend it."

"Skating is for ice-rinks in the city," Erica said with conviction. "No worries I'd try it on a *pond*."

Drew only smiled as she sliced the potatoes Erica had peeled. She understood Erica's wonder at their surroundings, although her daughter always had a sassy way of putting things. A year ago, Drew would never have believed she'd be living in this beautiful place doing this much cooking, from scratch, for a B&B full of guests as well as a big family of her own.

She hadn't realized people would actually book for Christmas, but they were full. The Bluebonnet Inn was gaining a reputation for a cozy, relaxing-but-elegant vacation spot, in an area filled with fishing, boating, hiking, and horseback riding. A wonderful get-away-from-the-rat-race hideaway.

The guests were joining the Malorys for one big Christmas dinner—that had been Ray's and Kyle's idea. Ray had realized he and Drew wouldn't be able to get away to the Malory ranch with all the guests they needed to attend to, but he'd also not felt right about shutting themselves up in a separate room for a private feast.

Kyle had been all for the combined meal. Much of his eagerness was because of Lucy, Drew understood. The brothers figured Lucy would feel less awkward if she wasn't the only person in the dining room without a plus-one.

The Malory brothers were tiptoeing around Lucy a bit too much, in Drew's opinion, but she kept that to herself. They loved their sister and worried about her. Anna had confided in Drew that she'd suggested Lucy invite Hal, but who knew how that would go?

Drew paused a moment to bask in the fullness of her life. Erica had blossomed from a resentful transplanted preteen into a full-fledged Riverbender, active in school life, riding in competitions, becoming fast friends not only with Faith and Dominic, but many others she'd met at school in the past year. She'd be dating soon, Drew thought with a pang.

Drew, who assumed she'd spend the rest of her life alone, had a supporting, caring husband who helped her without criticism and loved her without conditions. Drew caught Ray's arm as he passed her to get more plates and pulled him down for a lingering kiss.

Her hot cowboy cupped her face, his hand warm. He had such strength and yet he gentled it for her.

"Get a room," Erica said with a snicker.

Ray and Drew broke apart. Ray's hot smile made Drew buzz, but he joined in Erica's mirth.

"We have one," Ray said. "But we're a little busy right now."

"Yeah, we are." Erica returned to potato peeling with gusto, parings flying across the worktable. "This is going to be some party."

Ray reluctantly released Drew so she could continue chopping, for the mountain of mashed potatoes she'd make. He lingered in the kitchen, however, as though happy to stay in the cozy space with his new family.

Drew laid her knife aside. "I think this is a good time to give you both your Christmas gift."

"Ohh." Erica perked up. "More presents. I like it."

Ray turned a puzzled gaze to Drew. They'd exchanged gifts earlier this morning, Ray earning squeals from Erica with brand new riding boots, jacket, and hat. The lovely malachite earrings Ray had given Drew dangled from her ears even now.

Drew wiped her hands, folding them to face her husband and daughter, the two people she loved most in the world.

"Next Christmas we'll have one more at our party," she said, trying to stem her excitement. "He or she—don't know yet."

Both Erica and Ray stared at her, one pair of brown eyes and one green, wondering what she meant.

Then Erica dropped her peeler and threw her fists in the air. "Woo-hoo!" Her yell split the room. "About time! I told you guys I wanted a brother. Though I'll take a sister too."

Ray's face remained frozen as he blinked once, twice. A

slow flush rose up his cheeks at the same time a smile lifted his mouth.

"You sure?"

Drew nodded shakily. "Dr. Sue confirmed it at the clinic yesterday."

"Well, shit."

Usually Ray kept his language tame around Erica, but the word slipped out. Erica, laughing and dancing around the kitchen, never noticed.

Ray had once expressed the fear that he couldn't father children. At one time, Christina hadn't been certain whether her daughter, Emma, belonged to Ray or Grant, and Drew knew Ray had been somewhat crushed to find out he wasn't Emma's dad. He and Christina had already broken up and Christina had wanted to be with Grant, but the disappointment had still been a blow.

Drew watched hope and then profound happiness bloom in Ray's eyes. He closed the distance between him and Drew and crushed her in an embrace.

"Damn, that's good news." His warm breath brushed her ear. "Real good news."

Drew lifted her head. Tears stood in Ray's eyes, which brought them to Drew's. She touched his cheek.

"Merry Christmas, Ray."

Ray's answering kiss took her breath away. He held her tight, his mouth fierce as he kissed and kissed her. Drew hung on to her cowboy and enjoyed the ride.

Finally, Ray eased the kiss to its end, his eyes sparkling and his smile wide.

Erica danced near them, making hooting noises of joy. Drew held Ray's hands, so much love in her heart.

Ray dragged in a shaking breath. "I love you, Drew Paresky-Malory. Best. Christmas. *Ever*."

———

Lucy cheered with the rest of the crowd in the B&B's big front room at Drew's announcement. She rushed to them, throwing her arms around both her brother and Drew.

"I am so excited for you two!" Lucy crooned.

Ray had wanted this for a long time, Lucy knew. She loved Drew to pieces for making him so happy.

Others surged forward to congratulate Drew, including a few of her friends from Chicago, librarians all, who'd flown down to spend Christmas with Drew and Erica. Lucy eased away from the group, letting them surround Drew and Ray, their exclamations tinged with laughter.

Anna had been correct that Lucy wouldn't feel left out with all these people here, some single, some couples, one pair of sisters grabbing relaxation time over the holidays. Lucy was glad she'd come now, though there was one large absence. She'd not seen or heard a thing from Hal. When she'd asked Ray, oh so casually, whether Hal would be joining them, Ray had only shrugged and said he didn't know.

Lucy decided she'd have some dinner, drink a glass of wine, help Drew with whatever she needed, and then say good-bye and go home. Her excuse would be that she had to assist Anna tomorrow. No time off for the vets.

She turned to begin a conversation with one of the Chicago guests when the front door opened, leaking a chill but welcome breeze through the crowded and overheated room.

A low, rumbling voice said, "Hey."

He directed the word to Ray, who'd come forward to greet him. Hal held a box from Grace's bakery, which he handed to Ray, but his eyes went to Lucy and remained there.

Lucy, her heart hammering, found herself moving in his direction. She might just stay longer after all.

CHAPTER ELEVEN

Yes, Dale would have loved this.

Olivia Campbell gazed down the table at her large family—five sons, five daughters-in-law, and all her grandchildren.

The dining room was total chaos, with many conversations going at once. Dominic shouted across at Faith, her high-pitched voice answering. The ladies laughed and chattered, the sons conducting mock arguments or booming with laughter. Ross waving for Grant's attention—"Can I have the salt, for the fourteenth time, big bro?"

Carter soft-punched Grant on the arm, grabbed the saltshaker that was planted in front of Grant, and passed it to his favorite little brother.

"Hey, I was getting there," Grant protested.

"Next year, maybe," Carter returned.

He and Grant exchanged growls that dissolved into chortles.

At Olivia's side, Sam joined in the conversations with

plenty of opinions or agreements, and laughed along with everyone.

He belongs here.

The thought didn't come to Olivia as a jolt, but with a quiet conviction, a surety. Sam was a part of Olivia's life, one she didn't want to lose.

Sam caught Olivia's gaze. His instant smile flashed fire through her, one she'd never thought she could feel again.

No more uncertainty. Sam reached over and squeezed her hand then went back to his argument with Adam over where the best fish in the region could be found.

"On a plate, in a restaurant," Tyler yelled from down the table, and laughter drowned further words.

Once everyone had eaten their fill—including as much of Grace's pumpkin pie, sweet potato pie, and her tall cake slathered with orange-scented whipped cream as they could—Ross rose, grabbed dishes, and started carting them to the kitchen.

"We got this," Tyler declared as he followed suit. "Right guys?"

"Right." Grant stacked plates. "Ladies, go drink wine in the living room. You've done enough."

"I think I'm in love," Christina crooned. She slid one arm through Bailey's, the other through Jess's, and towed them out of the dining room, Callie happily following.

Grace, who could never let go of the kitchen, hovered, but Carter and Faith shooed her away.

When Sam started to help, Adam snatched the plates from his hands. "You're a guest. Go do guest things. Mom, take him out of here."

Sam threw up his hands in resignation. "All right, all right. Liv, let's go."

He slid his arm around Olivia's waist and led her, not to the living room, but out to the long veranda at the back of the house. The sun was shining, the afternoon turning warm, the quiet restful after the roar inside.

Sam released Olivia and rested his elbows on the porch railing, the two of them gazing across the land that fell away from the rear of the house. On the lower slope, several years ago now, Bailey and Adam had married.

"Good memories," Olivia said.

"The best."

The sun made crimson streaks in the western sky, a fine day ending. Olivia leaned next to Sam. "I thought I wouldn't want to stay here after Dale went, but now the good memories outweigh the bad. They always will, I think."

"I think you're right," Sam answered.

They'd both seen so much, had lost much, and had grieved deeply. And yet Olivia knew she'd been given a precious gift—life in this home with a family that loved unwaveringly.

"You're a part of my world, Sam," Olivia said.

Sam turned to her, sunlight dancing in his brown eyes. "You're a part of mine."

"One I don't want to let go."

"No."

A long time ago, Olivia might have launched into a speech about why they should stay together and see what life handed them. These days, she knew a lot of words weren't necessary. Something was meant to be, or it was not.

"Stay," Olivia said, very softly.

Sam regarded her quietly, the answer already in his eyes. He brushed a fingertip across her lips. "For always?"

"Yes." Olivia turned her head and kissed his palm.

A grin tugged at Sam's mouth. "Are you proposing to me, Olivia Campbell?"

"I think I am." Olivia's heartbeat quickened as she spoke the daring phrase. Sam might not want what she wanted. He might see them simply as friends helping each other through the loneliness.

Sam's eyes softened. "Then I think I'll say yes."

Olivia released her breath in a rush, a laugh coming with it. "That's a relief. I'd feel like such an idiot if you said no."

"You never can be." Sam clasped her hands and drew her close. "How about I be the idiot? Olivia Campbell, will you marry me?"

Sudden tears filled Olivia's eyes as happiness began to bubble deep inside her. The many, many long nights she'd spent alone, hiding her sorrows so her sons wouldn't worry, drifted away on the light Texas wind.

"I will, Sam Farrell."

"Good." Sam's eyes crinkled with his warm smile. "That's very good."

His lips were hot on hers as he pulled her into a kiss, the touch promising more of the passion they'd barely tasted.

A whoop broke the peaceful quiet. On the other side of

the large back window, Grant held up a champagne bottle, Olivia's other four sons and their wives and kids crowding behind him. Everyone was grinning, Faith bouncing on her toes.

"I'd say this calls for a celebration," Grant yelled. He popped the cork with a bang that made everyone jump, and champagne frothed over his hands. "Let's grab something to catch this mess." Christina thrust glasses under the deluge, which calmed as Grant began to pour.

The back door opened, Olivia's family flooding out and around her, embracing her and Sam, welcoming him into the fold.

The wind strengthened as the laughter and voices rose, flowing over the grasslands that was the Hill Country, swirling through the entirety of the Circle C Ranch, as though knowing it was whole again.

AUTHOR'S NOTE

Thank you for reading! I am happy to have had the chance to revisit Riverbend and the Campbell and Malory families.

I've always wanted Olivia, matriarch of the Campbell family—to find her own happily ever after. I also wanted Sam Farrell, uncle to Christina and Bailey, to find happiness, and I decided the two would be perfect together. It was also great to revisit the various families and see what they were up to.

Lucy and Karen will each have their tales told. Lucy's story, Riding Hard: Hal is next, followed by Karen's story: Riding Hard: Jack.

If you are new to the Riding Hard series, the best place to start is with Book 1, *Riding Hard: Adam*. The series continues through the five Campbell brothers and then the Malory family.

I hope you enjoyed this jaunt to Riverbend, and Happy Holidays!

ALSO BY JENNIFER ASHLEY

Riding Hard

(Contemporary Romance)

Adam

Grant

Carter

Snowbound in Starlight Bend

Tyler

Ross

Kyle

Ray

A Riverbend Christmas

Shifters Unbound

(Paranormal Romance)

Pride Mates

Primal Bonds

Bodyguard

Wild Cat

Hard Mated

Mate Claimed

"Perfect Mate" (novella)

Lone Wolf

Tiger Magic

Feral Heat

Wild Wolf

Bear Attraction

Mate Bond

Lion Eyes

Bad Wolf

Wild Things

White Tiger

Guardian's Mate

Red Wolf

Midnight Wolf

Tiger Striped

(novella)

A Shifter Christmas Carol

Iron Master

Last Warrior

Shifter Made ("Prequel" short story)

ABOUT THE AUTHOR

New York Times bestselling and award-winning author Jennifer Ashley has more than 100 published novels and novellas in romance, urban fantasy, mystery, and historical fiction under the names Jennifer Ashley, Allyson James, and Ashley Gardner. Jennifer's books have been translated into more than a dozen languages and have earned starred reviews in *Publisher's Weekly* and *Booklist*. When she isn't writing, Jennifer enjoys playing music (guitar, piano, flute), reading, hiking, and building dollhouse miniatures.

More about Jennifer's books can be found at
http://www.jenniferashley.com

To keep up to date on her new releases, join her newsletter here:
http://eepurl.com/47kLL